Deadly Deception

By the same author

EVIL STREAK

UNWILLINGLY TO SCHOOL

DESERVING DEATH

DEADLY OBSESSION

VENGEANCE DEFERRED

Deadly Deception

Peter Conway

ROBERT HALE · LONDON

First published in Great Britain 2009

ISBN 978-0-7090-8931-5

Robert Hale Limited
Clerkenwell House
Clerkenwell Green
London EC1R 0HT

www.halebooks.com

2 4 6 8 10 9 7 5 3 1

Typeset in 11/18pt New Century Schoolbook
Printed in Great Britain by the
MPG Books Group, Bodmin and King's Lynn

CHAPTER ONE

JAMES COCHRANE, NOT for the first time in the preceding few months, hadn't slept well. Soon after 6 a.m. when it was getting steadily lighter, it was a relief to get up. He pulled back the curtains in his small single bedroom and looked out over the garden at the rear of the house near the Roehampton Gate leading to Richmond Park.

He stretched and threw open the window, savouring the crisp early morning air, the birdsong and the view of the extensive back garden of the five-bedroomed 1930s house. Through the screen of trees behind the large lawn, he could just make out his pride and joy, the large wooden summer house, which was his refuge from all the domestic and hospital stresses. He had taken up calligraphy several years earlier and not only had it provided a relaxation, but he discovered that he had a real talent both for it and for design.

It was with a deep sense of anticipation that he looked forward to working on the book plate that was his latest project. Cochrane was a methodical, mildly obsessive man, though, and didn't hurry his usual Sunday morning ritual of shower, meticulous shave with his cut-throat razor, breakfast of half a grapefruit, boiled egg, toast and marmalade. After he had washed up, he made his bed, which had been thoroughly aired with the sheet and blanket pulled back and the cool breeze playing on it through the wide-open window.

There were no sounds coming from the rest of the house as he made his way out of the back door along the path by the side of the lawn and through the line of trees beyond it. Between that and the fence that separated the property from the one behind was a substantial area which was partly grassed and contained the summerhouse to the left and a large swimming pool, with a tiled surround, on the other. Between them, right at the back of the garden, was the goldfish pond with a small island of rocks in the middle of it, on which was an ornamental fountain, which he liked to watch from the side window of his hut, when he was resting his eyes at intervals while working on his designs.

Another part of his Sunday morning ritual was to feed the goldfish. He unlocked the door of the summerhouse, picked up the rubber mat inside and the packet of seed from one of the shelves and knelt down on the mat placed on one of the flat stones that surrounded the pond. He was just about to sprinkle a pinch of the fish food on to the water, when there was a blinding flash of light in front of his eyes and he pitched forward.

It was about an hour and a half later that Miles Howarth, whose garden backed on to that of James Cochrane, was emptying some kitchen waste on to his compost heap, when over the fence he saw that the door of his neighbour's hut was open. He had been meaning to tell the man of his plans to pollard some of his trees, the branches of which were overhanging and getting perilously close to the top of the fence and this seemed as good a time as any to tell him about it.

'James!' he called loudly. 'Could you spare a moment?'

When there was no reply, with considerable difficulty he climbed on to the brick surround of the compost heap and looked over the fence. James Cochrane was lying with his head under the water of the goldfish pond and the water was stained with blood.

Howarth was seventy-five, had severe arthritis of both hips and he knew immediately that there was no way that he was going to be able to climb over the fence and he moved back towards his house as fast as he could in a travesty of a run, where he rang for an ambulance. It took him less than five minutes to get into his car and drive the few hundred yards into the parallel road behind, where he pulled up outside Cochrane's property. He pressed the bell on the front door and hammered on it with the handle of his stick. It seemed an eternity before he heard the window on the floor above being opened and, looking up, he saw the tousled head of a teenage boy, whom he presumed to be Cochrane's son, peering out.

'I live in the house directly behind this one,' he said, raising his voice, 'and I saw over the fence that Dr Cochrane's had an accident near the goldfish pond and he's unconscious. I've already sent for an ambulance and I'd like to see if there's anything else I can do. Is your mother here?'

'Yes, but I'm not sure if she's woken up yet. She likes to sleep late on Sundays.'

'In that case, after you've let me into the back garden, perhaps you'd let her know what's happened and then wait outside for the ambulance and show the crew the way?'

The boy nodded. 'There's a gate between the house and the garage, which isn't bolted and you could get in that way.'

As Howarth was making his way painfully across the lawn, he heard the high-pitched scream coming from one of the upstairs rooms in the house behind him. He had served in the army in Northern Ireland forty years earlier for quite long enough to know when someone was dead and Cochrane was certainly that. The back of the man's head was covered with blood and he was unable to feel any pulses coming from either side of his neck. Deciding not to disturb anything else, he took his mobile phone, which he had picked up from the hall table before leaving his house, out of his pocket and this time rang for the police.

'Tyrrell!'

The Detective Chief Superintendent stopped abruptly and turned to see Brian Rogers, one of the Assistant Commissioners, standing at the entrance to his office.

'May I have a word with you?'

'Of course, sir.'

'You may have seen in the papers about the death of one of

the psychiatrists at the Henshaw Hospital last Sunday when he was found dead in his back garden,' the man said when Tyrrell was sitting in front of his desk.

'Yes, sir, I did.'

'I gather from the preliminary report of the forensic pathologist that the man was certainly murdered and an ex-colleague of mine, now retired, is on the board of governors of the hospital and thinks someone senior ought to take the case over. Evidently this man, Cochrane, has been in conflict with one of the other consultants recently and I gather that there have been rumours that he was thinking of taking an action against her for libel. It seems that the woman wrote an article in one of the psychiatric journals recently, virtually accusing the man of malpractice with regard to the management of ME. I have heard of the condition, of course, but am not up to speed on the details. Anyway, after discussing it with Tredgold and the local officers who went to the house in response to the 999 call, I am convinced that we do need someone of your seniority to take the case over and, what's more someone with experience in the handling of medical personnel and the press, for that matter.

'According to Tredgold, the female psychiatrist is a tricky customer and he thinks that having a woman on the team is essential, which is the reason why your name and that of your two assistants came up. I'd like you to put them on to it right away and keep a watching brief yourself. We have already obtained a search warrant for the man's house, but I leave it to your judgement to decide whether or not to get everyone to leave. Cochrane also had an office at the hospital; I have arranged for the inner one, where he kept his personal records, to be sealed, but after consultation with the chairman of their medical committee, the outer one, where his secretary works, has been left open, so that she can answer inquiries about patients. He also knows that we will be interviewing some of the staff.'

Tyrrell nodded. 'I know a little about ME. As it is much more common in females than males and affects predominantly teenagers and young people, and from what you've said about the female psychiatrist, I fully agree with Tredgold that it's essential to have a woman working on this case. I'll get on to it straight away.'

'Good man, I knew I could rely on you. I've already cleared it with the local force. Keep me posted, will you?'

'Of course, sir.'

Tyrrell had been able to arrange an urgent appointment for his two assistants, Inspectors Sarah Prescott and Mark Sinclair, to see Douglas Metcalfe, the chairman of the academic board of the Henshaw Hospital and the two of them met him early that afternoon.

'It's very good of you to come so quickly,' the man said after the introductions had been made. 'Naturally, after the tragedy of Dr Cochrane's death, I have had to cancel the staff meeting that was due to be held this afternoon and I am in the process of rescheduling it for some time next week. I am not exactly looking forward to it, but at least after seeing you, if nothing else, I can justly claim to have taken some action over the incident, even if, as I'm sure you know, it was not entirely the result of any initiative on my part.'

Sinclair nodded. 'Perhaps, as a start, you would give us an impression of the sort of person Dr Cochrane was?'

'He was very conscientious, very thorough and a very good medical doctor, but I have to say that he would have made a better neurologist than psychiatrist. He tended to be somewhat cynical with regard to the more fundamental forms of psychotherapy, particularly analysis, and favoured physical treatment, such as psychotropic drugs, occasional ECT for the very depressed and also behaviour therapy.'

'I understand that there was some conflict with one of his colleagues over ME.'

'That would be a considerable understatement. One of the other members of our staff, Dr Audrey Clements, has had what almost amounts to a mission to persuade the profession that ME has a physical cause and in 2002 had considerable support following a statement from the Chief Medical Officer that ME was a genuine and disabling condition. While not disputing that that was the case, Cochrane published a well-argued paper in which he made the point very forcibly that it was one thing to acknowledge its existence, but quite another to say that it was due to a physical agent such as a virus. Where, he asked was the virus, or any other agent for that matter? Making a diagnosis of ME was as good as saying that the medical profession had nothing to offer other than sympathy and tender loving care and waiting for it to get better over months or even years. Why were females more prone to it than males? Were there any parallels with anorexia nervosa? Surely, he suggested, it was better to continue to look for a cause and try different methods of treatment, rather than to say that rest, sympathy and time were the only options.

'Any suggested treatment needed to be assessed carefully and that most certainly included alternative methods, which had already entered the lists. There were also dangers in making the diagnosis uncritically as the symptoms could be the result of other dangerous and treatable physical and psychiatric conditions being missed. Only recently, he wrote, he had come across an adolescent who had been diagnosed with the condition, only for it to be discovered many months later that her lassitude and general weakness were due to a tumour of the pituitary gland and the delay in diagnosis and surgical removal of it had led to permanent visual defects due to pressure on the optic pathways.

'Dr Clements wrote a letter, which was published, saying that by denying the existence of ME, Cochrane was flying in the face of the evidence and the opinions of experts in the field, of which he clearly was not one. She didn't say in so many words that his misogynistic sentiments had clearly got the better of the evidence, his critical faculties and the duties expected of a caring professional, but those were the implications, however much they were obscured by the use of arcane language.

'Maybe I am overstating the libellous nature of that letter, but evidently Cochrane's lawyer didn't think so. Personally, I seriously doubt that the man had any real intention of suing, but Dr Clements was very worried about it and she has become very anxious and strident. One could say, therefore, that Cochrane's death has not been wholly unwelcomed in some quarters. There is one last joker in the pack. The daughter of Cochrane's wife by a former marriage, who lives with them, but was not formally adopted by him, has been diagnosed as having the condition and perhaps you have already divined that the young woman is under Dr Clements's care.'

'From what you've said already, that sounds very curious and even verging on the unethical. How did that situation arise?'

'Cochrane felt it was a great mistake to become involved in the medical management of any member of his family, particularly a girl who was neither his natural nor his adopted daughter, and he decided to leave it to the girl's mother and her GP, who had made the diagnosis originally. It was he who referred her to Dr Clements, knowing that she had written a good deal about the condition and that she was an acknowledged expert in the field. The patient, who was about eighteen when it started, was initially assessed as an in-patient, and I don't know what arrangements were made for her follow-up – you'd have to ask Dr Clements about that. I doubt if the girl's care would have been left entirely to the GP, not least because Dr Clements is, I believe, in the process of collecting data for a monograph on the subject. No doubt, though, the GP is coping with any day-to-day problems not directly associated with the condition.'

'Did Dr Cochrane have any other children?'

'I don't know. You see, although naturally I was on good terms with him and knew his professional work well, social contacts were another matter. That situation arises quite frequently in a specialist hospital like this one and, unlike in days gone by, social events organized for the staff no longer exist. If a colleague lives in a different part of London, particularly north of the river like me and south like Cochrane, and if one didn't train with them, then one has really no social contact at all.

'You might like to have a word with Walter Paterson, one of his colleagues here. He and Cochrane were contemporaries as students at St Gregory's Hospital, remained friends, and I'm sure he'd be prepared to have a chat with you. He's head of our clinical neurophysiology department and, although he has a medical degree, he does not practise clinical medicine. He's a thoroughly nice man and you'll be able to get a more unbiased view of Cochrane than from anyone else I can think of here. I'll give him a ring if you like. Knowing him, I'm sure he would be glad to fit you in straight away and, as his time is more flexible that that of the clinicians, it's not as if you would be interrupting any consultations with patients, unless, of course, he's carrying out a test on one himself.'

'Thank you, that would be most helpful.'

Walter Paterson was a powerfully built man wearing a slightly rumpled brown suit and looked to be in his early fifties.

'I gather that Metcalfe has already given you details of Cochrane's dispute with Audrey Clements,' he said.

'Yes, that's right,' Sinclair replied, 'but we would also like to hear from you anything you know about his personal life.'

The man nodded. 'I was friends with James Cochrane for the best part of thirty years. We trained at St Gregory's together and, while he eventually went into psychiatry, I took up clinical neurophysiology. Although our different postgraduate training meant that we went to separate centres initially, and as a result didn't see much of each other for a time, we never lost touch and both of us were delighted when we finished up here together some twenty years ago and we remained firm friends.

'His first wife, Julia, was a nurse at St Gregory's. She was a really lovely person and she and my wife also got on very well together. On a number of occasions the four of us went on holidays together and later on their daughter, Rebecca, was often round at our house as she and our daughter, Rachel, used to go riding together. Julia's death ten years or so ago was a terrible blow to all of us – she had bowel cancer that didn't respond to treatment. Rebecca, like her mother, is a very robust, direct sort of person and reacted positively, by being determined to get on with her life. She is also extremely bright and is currently one of the senior registrars in medicine at St Gregory's and, in my view is almost certain to get a consultant post there, or at another teaching hospital, in the next year or two.

'James, on the other hand, was always uxorious in the

extreme and took his wife's death very badly. He made the disastrous decision to marry Jean only eighteen months later. She could hardly have been more different from Julia. She needed high maintenance, was up and down, one minute hyperactive and over cheerful and the next depressed and full of woe. James was a thoroughly nice man, but had quite the wrong personality to cope with someone like her. What that woman needed was a kick up the backside from time to time, not unending sympathy and having her every whim satisfied.

'When Jean first came on the scene, we saw plenty of her, but it was not long before our social contacts diminished almost to nothing, although once or twice at weekends, Rebecca would pick James up and bring him over to our house for the day without Jean. To be honest, neither my wife nor I liked Jean and the last straw, as far as I was concerned, was the behaviour of her daughter by her first husband when we went to their house for tea one Sunday. Amy was about fifteen then and was extremely rude and petulant. After refusing James's very reasonable request for her to stop tapping her cup with a spoon when I was trying to engage her mother in conversation, she stormed out of the room, slamming the door behind her.

'In days gone by she might well have received a well-deserved warming of her backside with a hairbrush, but all Jean could find to say was, "poor dear, she is going through a difficult age just now". James apologized to me for the girl's behaviour and said how worried he was about her and didn't know what to do about the situation.

'Together with one of the boys, who was a bit older than her, she went on to be expelled from her private boarding school for drinking in a local pub, having sex and smoking cannabis. As every suggestion James made about her getting a job or going to a tutoring college in London was rejected, he decided to approach her natural father. That didn't work either, the man saying that he had a new young family of his own to worry about, that Amy had chosen to live with her mother and it was up to her to sort it out. James did get the young woman to start at a secretarial college, but not long after that she developed ME and got into the hands of Audrey Clements, which was a serious concern to him. He neither liked nor respected Audrey and I don't blame him in the least for refusing to have anything to do with the management of Amy's condition. Indeed, I think he was wise to keep well out of it.'

'Did the second Mrs Cochrane have any other children?' Sarah asked.

'Not of her own, but she and her first husband adopted David after she had had major gynaecological problems following Amy's birth and had to have a hysterectomy. David must be seventeen now and is rather like James was when I first knew him, being very bright, shy and obsessional. He is a computer geek, spending a lot of time playing chess on it, and has also an elaborate model train system up in the loft. James worried about him a lot and told me that he thought that he was mildly autistic, although the last thing he wanted was to put that label on him as it would make his life even more difficult than it was already. Evidently, right from the start the boy found his adoptive mother with her emotional incontinence deeply embarrassing and for some reason James felt that he had failed him in some way.

'That was typical of James and one of the reasons why I often wondered if psychiatry was the right speciality for him. It is always a mistake for doctors to take their patients' problems home with them, which he did, and that particularly applies to psychological medicine. Had he got the diagnosis right, was he handling the patient in the best way? Those were some of the issues that used to worry him and he was always agonizing about them. It was hardly surprising that these concerns should have applied to David and whether or not he should get one of his colleagues to see him.

'With James having gone, I can't help being very concerned about the boy. It was obvious that he and Amy were like chalk and cheese. Before she got ME she was always expecting him to help her with her coursework during her holidays from boarding school and also in the use of her laptop, which she found difficult to master. He always seemed to be at his mother's and Amy's beck and call until James insisted on the family having an au pair girl.'

'Do you know how the au pair girl coped with the situation?'

'I can't help you there. James did tell me that she was the daughter of an old French friend of his and unlike a couple of others that they had had, both of whom had left after a matter of weeks, the new girl knew exactly how to handle Jean. She was sympathetic and helpful, particularly with Amy, but also quite firm, making the young woman get dressed properly and taking her for walks round the garden if the weather was fine. How she managed to achieve that I'll never know, when Amy spent the rest of her time slumped either in bed or in an easy chair in her bedroom, either listening to her music system, watching TV or immersed in *Hello* magazine.

'I gathered that in return for being on hand at night except at the weekends, the au pair girl was given plenty of time to herself during the week. It sounded to me to have been quite a good deal for her, because she made friends with a near neighbour's daughter and used to go up to London, riding in the park and swimming in the pool with her in the back garden of James's house. James told me that he liked the girl, that she was always cheerful and pleasant and was patient with his attempts at speaking his rather rusty French with her, although her English was perfectly adequate and she was obviously keen to learn to speak it better. He had hoped that Amy might take the opportunity to learn some spoken French, too, but, not surprisingly, that didn't work as she was unable to concentrate as the result of her illness!'

'How did David get on with the au pair?' Sinclair asked.

'I only met the girl once when I went back to the house with James after a game of golf one weekend and she brought the drinks out into the garden. David was also there and he gave the impression of being terrified of her. She was only with us for a matter of minutes and when she gave the poor fellow a look, raised her eyebrows and leaned forward to hand him his drink, he blushed scarlet as he clearly had a view of all there was to see under the loose shirt she was wearing, which was not covered by a bra, and it was quite obvious that he hardly knew what to do with himself.'

'Is the girl still there?'

'I don't know.'

'Well, thank you. What you have said makes Cochrane's domestic situation much clearer and that should make things easier for us when we visit the house in Roehampton and I am most grateful to you.' The man inclined his head slightly. 'Do you have any further questions, Sarah?'

She nodded. 'I wonder if you would tell us where you stand on the issue of ME.'

The man gave a rueful smile. 'I'm no clinician and all I can say is that the muscle and nerve tests I have carried out on those affected by the condition have proved to be normal apart from the patients clearly not exerting maximum effort.'

'You mean that they were not trying?'

'There lies one of the cruxes of the problem. There are those that believe that that is the case; others, like Dr Clements, believe that those tests are very blunt instruments and that the patients have subtle abnormalities of the brain due to the agent causing the disease and, as a result, are incapable of making the effort. I hope that makes some sort of sense to you.'

Sarah nodded. 'One last question. Can you think of any reason why anyone would want to kill Dr Cochrane?'

'Well, any psychiatrist who habitually deals with unstable, unhappy and sometimes psychotic patients is at some risk of physical attack, but that must be very rare, although I can't quote specific figures. It would clearly be totally unrealistic to deny that James had both professional and domestic problems, but in my view, he was not the type of person to provoke strong emotions, let alone homicidal ones. Having said that, though, if there is no doubt, as seems to be the case, that he was murdered, then someone must have hated or feared him enough to have done it. I gather that there is no possibility of his death having been accidental.'

'No, there isn't.'

'While we are here, why don't we try to get a feel for this Dr Clements, who appears to be a somewhat of a pivotal figure in all this?' Sinclair said when they were out in the corridor.

'I'm not sure about that and I wonder if it would be wise,' Sarah replied. 'She sounds to be a somewhat spiky character and I don't think it would be good tactics to tackle her until we find out a bit more about the sort of person she is.'

'Don't worry, I shall be the very soul of discretion.'

'That'll be the day.'

Sinclair looked at her severely. 'You surely know by now what happens to naughty young women who mock their elders.'

'I'm glad to hear that you left out the betters bit. Anyway, I can't wait.'

The two detectives had to wait for a good forty-five minutes before the psychiatrist marched into the room where they had been waiting. It would have been a major understatement to say that she looked irritated as they introduced themselves; she was positively bristling.

'Is it really necessary to interrupt my clinic when I have patients waiting to see me?'

Sinclair raised his eyebrows slightly. 'The reason we are here is on account of a patient of yours, one Amy Moffatt. We were hoping to get your advice about the best way to handle her and the situation facing her at home in the light of her mother's husband having been murdered. However, if you haven't time now, we'll just have to do the best we can under the present circumstances as the matter requires urgent action.'

Sarah saw the look of apprehension, almost of panic, as Sinclair made a move as if he was about to get to his feet.

'Just a moment,' the woman said, getting up and going through the communicating door to the adjacent room, returning almost at once. 'I'm sorry I was so short with you just now; I am under considerable strain at the moment. Not only do I have patients to see, but there is also a very difficult meeting of the medical staff coming up soon and that is very much on my mind just now. If James Cochrane was murdered, there are people who are going to suggest that I had some responsibility for it, but that would be both ridiculous and grossly unfair. I just thought that his views on ME were wrong and misguided, that's all.

'Naturally I am worried about the effects this tragedy will have had on Amy, but I should point out that she's not Cochrane's natural daughter and chose not to be adopted by him, either. I have not seen her myself for some weeks now and for that reason I suggest that you have a word with my senior registrar, Andrew Clarke. Amy's GP has been dealing with any day-to-day health problems not related to her ME and luckily she has been fortunate in that regard recently. Andrew has been monitoring her condition by carrying out roughly fortnightly domiciliary visits and supervising her nutrition and the gentle graded exercises needed to keep her joints mobile.'

'Thank you. In that case, we would like to see Dr Clarke and look forward to discussing the problems with you later.'

They only had to wait for ten minutes or so before the senior registrar was free. He proved to be extremely good-looking and didn't he know it, Sarah thought, as he greeted them with a broad smile and shook hands with both of them. He was a good six feet two in height, well-built, with dark hair and soft brown eyes, and she guessed that he was probably in his early thirties. He also had a way of looking at her in a slightly quizzical fashion, which threatened to defeat her determination not to blush.

'How do you think Amy is going to react to Dr Cochrane's death?' she asked, after the introductions had been made.

'My gut feeling is relief, once the initial shock has worn off. That must sound more than a bit harsh and cynical, but Amy never got on with Cochrane and indeed refused to be adopted by him. Part of the trouble, I believe, was that he felt more responsible for the boy that his wife and former husband had adopted, although that's not to say that he got on that well with him, either. I gather that the original idea of Amy's parents was to provide her with a brother, but it didn't work out like that at all, hardly surprising in my view. The boy was eleven when they took him on, had spent all his life in either institutions or foster homes, and had no social skills at all. He is undoubtedly clever, but he has never developed socially, is insecure in situations in which he has to meet strangers and spends most of his time with his laptop or in the attic playing with his model train set which Cochrane bought for him. As for Amy, according to Mrs Cochrane, she looked upon him as an interloper right from the start, which was hardly surprising as she was fifteen at that time and had clearly been spoiled by her mother. She also had nothing in common with the geek of a boy of eleven who suddenly appeared. Although shy herself, she had the usual teenage interests in fashion and pop music and both these were anathema to David, who liked nothing better than to be working away at the solitary pursuits I mentioned.

'Cochrane evidently used to get irritated by Amy's refusal to buckle down to her schoolwork and the last straw as far as he was concerned was when she was expelled from her private boarding school. I only ever heard Amy's side of that and she claimed that it was just for having been caught smoking cannabis on one occasion. At least that was her version of it, backed up by her mother, but I'm not sure I believed her. I learned very early during my visits to the house that Amy could be quite provocative physically, which is why I never saw her on my own, usually having the au pair girl present as well. Dr Clements herself had done all the initial assessment both at the first consultation and also on the only occasion when she was admitted to the ward, but later on, when she returned home, I concentrated on her physical well-being. It is easy to get the wires crossed if there is committee management of the psychiatric aspects of patients like Amy, which is why I kept away from that side of it and it was something that Dr Clements always insisted on.'

'Do you not take on the full management of cases like that yourself, then?' Sarah asked.

'Yes, I do, but my senior colleague is always there should I be concerned about some specific aspect of it and the best line to take.'

'Is that aspect reciprocal?'

'No, it isn't. Dr Clements and I don't have that sort of professional relationship.'

'Does she not discuss her cases with senior colleagues, either?'

'Certainly not where ME is concerned. Dr Clements is preparing a monograph on the condition and is very concerned that her original ideas on the subject might be leaked before publication.'

'So you don't know what these ideas are?'

'Of course, I am well aware of her general views on the subject, but not about her most recent thinking about it.'

'You must have seen a certain amount of Mrs Cochrane; how do you suppose she is going to cope with her husband's murder?' Sarah asked.

'I can't say that I know her that well and it's very difficult to say. She is obviously rather an emotional person and may fall apart completely, but sometimes people like her surprise one by finding their feet and coping well. It can't be denied that there were stresses in her marriage and, in situations like that, when a spouse dies one finds that there may be a mixture of guilt and relief and one is never sure which of those is going to predominate.'

'What do you suppose will happen with regard to Amy's management now?'

'In the short term, it may be necessary to take her into hospital for a time, although I don't think that would be in her interests at present and should be avoided if at all possible. She is beginning to show signs of improvement and we don't want her to become any more dependent than she is already. We also have to hope that the au pair girl doesn't up sticks and return to France. She is very good with Amy, much better than her mother, who not surprisingly has found the whole situation extremely stressful. In fact, I doubt if the au pair will leave; she is paid well over the odds and seems happy enough. At least, Mrs Cochrane has plenty of money, which may make things easier.'

'I understand that Cochrane had a natural daughter with his first wife.'

'Yes, but I've never met her and I haven't exactly been encouraged by my esteemed boss to fraternize with the enemy, as she sees it.'

'It was as bad as that, was it?'

The man smiled. 'One could say that.'

'Are you planning to see Amy again in the near future, now that all this has happened?' Sinclair asked.

'That will depend on Dr Clements.'

'Was anyone else here directly involved with Amy's management when she was an in-patient here?'

'Just our registrar, Alison Prior, who was our senior house officer at that time. She worked mainly on the ward then, took Amy's history and did the physical examination when the girl was admitted here for her initial assessment.'

'Is Dr Prior here today?'

'Yes, she is. Now, if you'll excuse me, I really must go; I still have patients to see and it's getting late.'

The man gave them both a smile, got to his feet, shook hands with them and left the room without looking back.

'Well,' Sinclair said, when Dr Clarke had closed the door behind himself, 'I must say I rather took to him. Does he, though, share his boss's views on ME? I just wonder.'

'So do I.'

'While we're here, perhaps we ought to have a word with the registrar, Alison someone, wasn't it?'

Sarah smiled. 'Prior. You and names – typical male.'

CHAPTER TWO

Alison Prior was still seeing patients in the clinic and they decided to have a sandwich and a coffee in the visitors' canteen.

'Overpriced and pretty unappetizing,' Sinclair said, looking at the dry-looking tuna and limp lettuce in the sandwich. 'I hope the patients on the ward do better, but I doubt it somehow from what I've heard about hospital food.'

They met the registrar in the sister's office in the adolescent unit on the third floor in the early afternoon. Alison Prior was a tall, thin and anxious-looking young woman in her middle to late twenties. She was wearing a skirt and blouse and looked tired, tense and drawn.

'I see that the nurses up here appear to have given up wearing uniforms now. Is that a recent change?' Sarah asked.

'No, that happened some years ago at Dr Clements's suggestion and I'm not entirely convinced that it was such a good idea.'

'Why's that?'

'Some of the patients take advantage of it. A few weeks ago

I saw one of the nurses helping an adolescent boy to put his shoes and socks on, while he was sitting on the side of his bed. He was perfectly capable of doing it himself and when she had gone, I told him off and asked him why he was being so lazy when the whole point of him being on the ward was to get him going again following a depressive illness.

'He gave me a cheeky grin and said: "I like looking down her blouse." The stupid girl wasn't wearing a bra and who could blame him?'

'Did you do anything about it?'

'I mentioned it to Dr Clements, saying that surely it was important for the nurses, if not to wear uniform, at least to dress appropriately.'

'What was her reaction?'

'She was most dismissive, saying that we are in the twenty-first century and the days of Florence Nightingale are long over.'

'Tell me about Amy Moffatt.'

'I must be very careful what I say, because I have my future career to think about, but I believed that she was exaggerating her symptoms when I first saw her about eighteen months ago. I was the senior house officer at that time and did the initial physical examination when she was admitted here. However, in view of who she was, Dr Clements covered the psychological side and kept her notes separately.'

'Surely that's most unusual.'

'Yes, it is, but then everybody here knew that Dr Cochrane was married to Amy's mother and that he didn't believe ME was a physical illness, and Dr Clements didn't want the risk of anyone reading her notes, which she kept locked up in her office.'

'Did Dr Cochrane visit Amy when she was on the ward?'

'Yes, he did, just the once. According to the nurse, Amy was perfectly horrid to him and Dr Clements told me to tell Dr Cochrane that it would be best if he didn't come again until she had settled in properly.'

'Why didn't she do that herself?' Sarah asked.

'The two of them didn't get on.'

'How did he react when you saw him?'

'He was most kind and told me not to worry or be embarrassed as he understood the situation perfectly. He also told me that Amy was a very vulnerable young woman and he was reassured to find that someone like me, who was not all that much older than her, was involved with her care and understood the pressure she was under.'

'What are your own views about ME?' Sinclair asked.

'I still haven't had enough experience to be able to make a clear judgement; just let me say that it strikes me as a dangerous diagnosis to make without very careful consideration. You see, similar symptoms can occur in other more treatable conditions and missing them can be disastrous.'

'Are you planning to continue in child and adolescent psychiatry?'

'No. I'm on the registrar rotation scheme now and I'm only doing six months on this firm, after which I intend to concentrate on adults.'

'And you'll be glad be moving on?'

The young woman pressed her lips together before answering. 'My present experience is proving most valuable and the only way to discover if one has a bent for any particular branch of psychiatry is to try a number of them out.'

'Did you ever work on Dr Cochrane's firm?' Sarah asked.

'Yes, I had six months on it as a registrar before coming on to this one.'

'And was his approach more to your liking?'

'Yes. He was an excellent general physician as well as a psychiatrist. He believed in physical methods of treatment and was extremely good with patients with anxiety states and depression.'

'What exactly do you mean by physical treatments?'

'Oral medication for the depressed and electroconvulsive therapy for those seriously affected, antipsychotic medication for those with schizo-affective disorders, and cognitive psychotherapy for the seriously anxious. That sort of thing.'

'Tell me about Amy.'

'Her GP referred her to Dr Clements because he thought she was suffering from ME. When she was admitted here, I did the initial physical examination, as I did on all the patients coming into the ward, but Dr Clements told me not to go into the psychological side as she intended to do that herself. I knew at once that there were going to be problems. Everyone here was aware of Dr Cochrane's reservations about the condition and I thought it tactless in the extreme for her GP to have referred the young woman here when it was only too obvious that there was ill feeling between the two of them, but perhaps he wasn't aware of that. I know that strictly speaking Amy wasn't related to Dr Cochrane, but he was married to her mother and she was living in the same house as he was.'

'You said earlier that when you saw Amy for the first time on the ward, you weren't able to assess her psychological state at all. Have you been able to get a view of it on this admission?' There was a very long pause. 'If you're worried about anything you say getting back to your superiors, I guarantee that it will be absolutely confidential,' Sarah said.

The young woman looked at the detective very directly and then nodded. 'Amy's management here worried me right from the start. She was certainly pale and underweight then, but my impression that she wasn't trying when I tested the strength of her muscles was borne out by the electromyographic tests. There was something else that worried me even more. Shortly after her admission, Dr Clements spent a long time with Amy on her own. There is nothing wrong with that, but Amy was in an extremely distressed state directly afterwards and I asked her what was the matter.'

There was another even longer long pause with the young doctor holding her lips tightly closed and then she took a deep breath and continued.

'I knew perfectly well then that my future career in psychiatry would be to a considerable extent dependent on what Dr Clements had to say about me and that, to my shame, is why I didn't take more action than I did. However, after Dr

Cochrane's murder, that no longer applies. Amy told me that Dr Clements had carried out a full physical examination of her in addition to the one I had already done, with the addition of an internal one – I expect you know what I mean by that – without the presence of a nurse. That is something which, at best, is unwise in the extreme, even if the examiner is another woman.'

'Had you ever known that to happen here before on a girl of Amy's age?' Sarah asked.

'No. There are strict guidelines about such a thing in most hospitals and certainly here. Firstly, it has to be essential and, if so, carried out by a gynaecologist or a veneriologist, and preferably a female one at that. I would never dream of doing such a thing myself and if there were special circumstances that made that examination urgent and essential, I would always have a nurse in attendance.'

'Do you know if Dr Clements had done anything like that before?'

'Certainly not on the wards during the two spells I worked for her here.'

'What are the indications for an examination like that?'

'Specific symptoms suggesting the possibility of a venereal infection or some gynaecological problem. Tests such as cervical smears also require it, but that would be undertaken by the appropriate specialist – a psychiatrist should never do it.'

'And there were no such symptoms in Amy's case?'

'No. She did admit to me that she had been expelled from her school for taking cannabis and having sex with a boy, but she told me that that was all over and at the time she had been checked at an STD clinic.'

'Did you let anyone else know about what Dr Clements had done?'

'I felt I had to tell someone and Dr Cochrane, on whose firm I had just finished, was the only person I could think of in whom I could confide. Also, even though she was neither his natural daughter nor had he adopted her, they were living under the same roof and I'm quite sure he felt considerable responsibility for her.'

'What was his reaction when you told him?'

'He told me that I had done the right thing in informing him about what had happened, said that he would deal with the matter himself and that I wasn't to worry about it.'

'Did he say whether or not he was going to tackle Dr Clements?'

'No.'

'And do you think he did?'

'I'm quite sure that he wouldn't have left something like that in abeyance.'

'When exactly did all this happen?'

'About a year ago. It was when I was finishing my time as an SHO and just before I became a registrar.'

'We know that Dr Clarke has been doing regular domiciliary visits to see Amy. Is that a common feature of management in ME?'

'Dr Clements thinks it's important in some cases and Amy's was one of them.'

'Do you agree with that?'

'Yes, I do. These patients do need to be followed up regularly and I don't think it's in their interests to have to attend out-patient clinics, with all the waiting about that that entails, not to mention the difficulties and expense of getting them here. Most of them need some form of transport such as a hospital car or ambulance.'

'How about Dr Clarke? Do you get on well with him?'

'I like him very much. He's an excellent teacher and he's always approachable if junior staff have any questions or difficulties.'

'Do you know what Amy thinks of him?'

'She gets on well with him and obviously both likes and trusts him.'

'Does he agree with Dr Clements's views on the nature and management of ME?'

'He's too tactful to say. I don't wish to sound too cynical, but let me just say that Dr Clarke needs her support if he is to get a good consultant post.'

'What is the plan for Amy now?'

'That will depend on Dr Clements and inevitably the awful news about Dr Cochrane is going to have a serious effect on the girl, even though she never got on with him.'

'Well, thanks for your help. What is the best way to get in touch with you should we need to do so again?'

'I carry a pager with me when I'm on duty here.'

'I presume you're not resident here any longer.'

'No, I'm not. I share a flat quite near here now with a girl who was at school with me. She works in public relations and is away most weekends. That suits me as I am working on a thesis for an MD degree at present.'

'That must be difficult on top of a demanding job.'

'It is, but it should be worth it in the long run. Dr Clements thinks it's a waste of time, but Dr Cochrane supported me all along and it was after discussions with him that I came up with the idea of a suitable subject.'

The two detectives arrived at Cochrane's house the following day an hour before their planned meeting with Jack Pocock, the head of the scene-of-crime team, and as they walked up towards the front door, it opened and a middle-aged man, carrying a black bag came out.

'Are you the family GP?' Sinclair asked, smiling at him.

'Yes, Ian Holmes. And you are?'

'I'm Inspector Mark Sinclair and this is my colleague, Inspector Sarah Prescott. We are from the CID and are beginning our investigation into this sad affair. Were you called in on the Sunday it happened?'

'I was indeed. Young David rang me soon after nine to say that his father had had an accident, that a neighbour had called an ambulance and that his mother had lost it completely, evidently screaming the place down, and that neither he nor the au pair girl knew what to do with her.

'By the time I got here, the ambulance had already arrived and the police were here as well. One of the officers told me that Cochrane was lying close to the goldfish pond at the back of the garden and that he had been dead for some time. The only way I was able to deal with Mrs Cochrane was to sedate her heavily and once I had made sure that the young people, Amy, David and the au pair girl, were all right, I decided to ring Cochrane's natural daughter, Rebecca and I stayed here until she arrived. She is a senior registrar in medicine at St Gregory's Hospital and I gather is expected to get a consultant post either there or at another London teaching hospital in the near future. She is a very calm and efficient young woman and said that she would deal with the situation. She told me that she was proposing to spend the night here and was hoping to get a few days' compassionate leave during the coming week and that she would do her best to sort things out.'

'Where is everybody at the present moment?'

'Mrs Cochrane was in such a state again this morning that I had to give her another sedative and she is now asleep, and Amy is sitting in her chair in her bedroom and seems quite calm. I think that Rebecca is with David in his bedroom and the au pair girl is in the kitchen.'

'Right. Thank you for your help.'

'That's all right. Rebecca has got my number if there are any further crises.'

Jack Pocock, who was carrying an attaché case, came out through the door between the garage and the house as the GP was leaving and the two detectives went towards him.

'That was the GP, Jack,' Sinclair said. 'Everything in the house seems under reasonable control and perhaps, first of all, you'd show us where the body was found?'

The scene-of-crime man nodded. 'There are three possible entries into the property, by the front door of the house, through the detached garage over there and by that gate between the two that I've just come through. That has not got a lock on it, but there is a thick bolt on the inside, which was not engaged and that was the way the man who found the body and the ambulance crew went into the back garden where the dead man was found. As for the garage, that has an electrically driven up-and-over door at the front, which can also be opened by a key and there is another entrance at the rear. Both of them were locked when I arrived. Keys for both of them were on the murdered man's ring in his trouser pocket.'

'Right, lead the way, Jack.'

There was a stone patio directly behind the house with access by French windows from the sitting room and it had a teak table and chairs set out on it. The lawn, with a path running along one side and flanked by flower beds, was roughly the size of a tennis court and at its end was a dense, neatly trimmed leylandii hedge, which hid the swimming pool, summerhouse and goldfish pond from view. The path at the side bypassed it and once they were in the area behind, which had been surrounded by tape, Pocock took several photographs out of his attaché case.

'This is the body as it was before Dr Tredgold got to work. The man who found it lives in the house directly behind that fence and his garden backs on to this one. He wanted to ask Cochrane about the branches of that tree there, which as you can see are overhanging the fence, as he wanted to pollard them. Seeing that the door of the summerhouse was open, he climbed on to the surround of his compost heap with a view to discussing it with the man and that's when he saw him lying face down in the water at the edge of the pond.

'The man has severe arthritis, knew that he wouldn't be able to climb over the fence and so drove round in his car. He hammered on the front door, the boy in the front bedroom heard him and after he had been told about Cochrane, the neighbour was directed through the side gate, which he was told was not bolted. The boy didn't come down himself, going to tell his mother what had happened. The man didn't move the body, merely feeling for the carotid pulses. He is a pretty cool customer and, having served as a colonel in the army in Northern Ireland years ago, is no stranger to violence of that sort. As you can see from the picture, Cochrane was lying face down in the water with evidence of a moderately severe injury to the back of his head and his position suggested that he was on his knees about to sprinkle some fish food on top of the water when he was hit from behind. His nose and mouth were under the water.'

'Any idea what was used to hit him?'

'To the side of the path we walked along just now we found the imprint of a sizeable stone that had been removed very recently – the earth there was still damp – and it seems possible that that was the murder weapon and, if so, Dr Tredgold might have found some earth in the wound to confirm it. So far, we haven't found any trace of the stone and

I suppose it's possible that it was taken away by the murderer or thrown over one of the fences.

'When we arrived, the summerhouse door was open and the unlocked padlock was hanging from the staple. Details of the prints and DNA on it are not yet available, but it seems reasonable to suppose that Cochrane had opened the door himself to get hold of the packet of fish food.' The SOCO reached into his case and produced a bunch of keys. 'These were in the man's trouser pocket and you might be interested to take a look at the summerhouse.'

Inside, there was an artist's table set against the side of the hut facing the swimming pool, which was parallel to it and separated from it by a grassed area. Set out on the table, which had a powerful adjustable light above it, was an unfinished design for a book plate, which was almost complete apart from the colouring.

'That's really beautiful work,' Sarah said. 'Did you find any others, Jack?'

'There are a few in that wooden cabinet over there.'

'I don't know a great deal about this sort of artwork,' Sinclair said when he had examined a couple of them, 'but I would guess that they are right up to professional standard. Find anything else, Jack?'

'Apart from pencils, pens, paper and various coloured inks, there was one rather curious object in the small fridge in addition to a couple of bottles of mineral water and some ice cream in the freezer. Dr Tredgold took it away, but I have a photograph of it.'

The picture showed a small bottle with what looked like blood in it and on the label it merely had a large 'X' written on it with the date of the Monday of the preceding week.

Before returning to the house, they took a brief look at the pool. It was roughly fifteen metres long by five wide with a springboard at one end covered by an electrically operated tarpaulin. There were four wooden folding loungers on the tiled surround.

'Quite some set-up,' Sinclair said. 'Right, we'd better talk to the people in the house. How about you, Jack?'

'I'm going to take a more careful look at the man's bedroom and study, which were secured during our first visit.'

There was also a key to the back door of the house, which led into the kitchen, on the bunch that Pocock had with him and as they went in they saw a tall, slim and elegant young woman, who looked to be in her late twenties, talking to a much younger one.

'Ah,' she said, 'you must be the two police officers.'

'That's right,' Sinclair said, showing her his warrant card, 'and I take it that you are Dr Cochrane's daughter, Rebecca.'

'You take it correctly,' she said, 'and this is Monique, who is the family's au pair girl and has been a tower of strength.'

'I imagine that Dr Paterson gave you a ring after our visit to the hospital.'

'That's right, he did.'

'May we offer you our condolences on the sad death of your father?'

'Thank you. Why not come in and I'll arrange for some coffee in the sitting room?'

'That would be very welcome,' Sinclair said, giving her a smile.

'Good. *Trois cafés et des biscuits au chocolat dans le salon, s'il te plaît*, Monique.'

The girl smiled at her and gave a little curtsy.

'I like to play that little game with Monique,' Rebecca Cochrane said when they were in the sitting room, 'even though her English is now much better than my French. It helped to break the ice when she first came here and we both enjoy playing that particular game. She's a great girl and has been worth her weight in gold.'

The room was large and close carpeted and contained a three-seat sofa, two armchairs, several bookcases and a grand piano in one corner.

'We were admiring the garden before when we came into the house. It must take some looking after,' Sinclair said.

'Yes, a man comes twice a week to deal with it. As you no doubt have already discovered, it extends quite a way behind those trees where there is a swimming pool and also a large summerhouse. It was originally intended as a changing room by the previous owners, but when Dad took over the house, he annexed it for his own use in order to get a bit of peace and quiet for his hobby of calligraphy. He was really good at it and designed cards, book plates and book marks. I have a key to the summerhouse as Dad let me use it for its original purpose so that I could have a swim when the family was away on holiday. That saved me going into the house and having to deal with the alarm system on it. With Amy's illness, though,

I haven't had the opportunity to take advantage of it this summer.'

'How did you get into the garden when they were away?'

'Through the garage. I have keys to both the up-and-over door at the front and also the one at the back.'

'Is that one normally kept locked?'

'Not when the family are here. David keeps his bicycle in the space behind Dad's and Jean's cars.'

'What about the gate between the garage and the house?'

'That's always bolted when they're away and that's why I have the keys to the garage. I don't know what's done about it when the house is occupied.'

'As you obviously know already, we have been to the hospital and seen your father's old friend, Dr Paterson, and Dr Metcalfe, the chairman of the academic board. We also had brief chats with those involved in Amy's care: Dr Clements, her senior registrar and the registrar,' Sarah said. 'It was made clear to us that there were tensions between Dr Clements and your father.'

'Yes, I know all about that. My father did discuss the whole business with me right from the beginning of Amy's problems and there has been a further recent development that may well shed light on his murder.'

'And what was that?'

'That Amy did not nor ever did have ME, or any other serious illness for that matter.'

'Perhaps you'd tell us why he believed that?'

'I will shortly, but first I should explain the situation here.

At the time of my father's death, those living here were my father, Jean, his wife, Amy Moffatt, her daughter, David her adopted son and Monique, the au pair girl. They all had separate bedrooms. Two of them, occupied by Jean and Amy, have en suite facilities, those used by David and Monique are quite a good size with basins in them and my father's is the smallest. There is also a third bathroom and lavatory.'

'Does the fact that your father and his wife didn't share a room mean that they weren't getting on?' Sarah asked.

'If you mean, were they no longer having sex, I don't know, but that arrangement certainly raises that possibility, though there may have been other explanations, such as snoring, restlessness and so on. How were they getting on? Not too well is the answer to that. My father should never have married Jean. She is a person who requires high maintenance, being extremely emotional, and is a great one for the grand gesture, whereas my father was serious-minded, appeared to be rather dull unless you knew him well and was very self-contained, not given to outward displays of emotion. That is not to say that he lacked feeling, he just didn't like to show it and he clearly found some of Jean's displays both distressing and difficult to handle.'

'Have you any close relatives on your father's side?'

'Only my grandmother, who has advanced Alzheimer's disease and is in a home in Derbyshire, close to where she used to live.'

'Did your father visit her regularly?'

'Yes, he did, pretty well every month and that concerned me.'

'In what way?'

'It's a long drive there and back and he had to stay the night at a bed and breakfast place close to the care home. Naturally, I respected his need to go there, but there's no point in pussyfooting about the issue. For a good two years my grandmother, who is now seventy-eight, has had not the slightest idea who she is, or where she is and she is almost mute. The last time I saw her with my father was nearly eighteen months ago and she didn't react to our visit at all, neither welcoming nor rejecting us with a single word, nor any change of expression. She was clearly being well cared for, and as tactfully as I could, I suggested to my father that regular visits did neither him nor her any good at all. More than that, she clearly found the appearance before her of a strange man unsettling and that distressed him.

'My father, as was his wont, respected my views and it was clearly not my place, once I had made the point to him, to go on about it. And so he continued to visit her regularly about once a month.'

'What about the financial aspects? Good care homes, like the one you describe, are very expensive and getting more so.'

'Luckily my grandfather was a senior civil servant and the fifty per cent of his pension which my grandmother gets as his widow covers the cost of her care comfortably. She also has some money of her own. That side of things has been in the hands of an accountant and her solicitor for some time now.'

'So you haven't seen your grandmother recently?'

'Not for about a year, when Dad was away at an overseas

conference, which was the last time I visited her. To be honest, I wasn't at all keen – it is a long way there and back in a day and I didn't want to spend the night there as I had work to do on my MD thesis. After my previous experience, I was well aware that it would be a complete waste of time, but I knew how much it would mean to him and so off I went. As I expected, my grandmother didn't react to my visit at all, just picking at the blanket over her knees without either saying a word or even looking in my direction. My father was embarrassingly grateful and I told a little white lie to the effect that my presence had seemed to calm the old lady a bit. I haven't seen her since, but my father always used to give me a report on his visits.

'Now, that's quite enough about me, and after we've had our coffee I suggest that we go up to see David. He is working in his room at the moment, but before we do so I think it would be sense to tell you something about him. He was adopted by Jean and her first husband, Malcolm Moffatt, after she failed to conceive again following Amy's birth. There were problems right from the start. Amy was fifteen when they made the decision and she deeply resented the arrival of an eleven-year-old boy. I have no idea why they waited so long or why they selected a child as old as David. It didn't help, either, that David should have been so much brighter than either Amy or his adoptive parents. Also, having been in a children's home for so long, he found it difficult, if not impossible, to fit into a family. It was not that he was particularly badly behaved; he just withdrew into his shell and, in truth, he has never managed to break out of it.

'I have no doubt that the divorce and Jean's marriage to my father, when he was thirteen, didn't exactly make things any easier, either for him or Amy. My father tried very hard to get to know the boy, encouraging him with his hobbies, helping him with his schoolwork and playing chess with him, but his efforts didn't really bear much fruit. David has a real talent for mathematics and science, but socially he is a disaster. He has no gift at all for making friends and when he was at a state school was a target for the bullies. Luckily, the private day school, where he is now, which my father found for him, is excellent. He appears to have fitted in well there and that side of things hasn't worked out badly at all.'

'You said hobbies. What were they?'

'Photography, his computer and model railway. Dad cleared out the loft for him, had it properly wired and put in lighting and heating. David wouldn't allow anyone, apart from Dad, up there, not that the rest of the family was the slightest bit interested and I'm sure Dad wasn't either, and as time went by, he rather gave up making the effort as David didn't appreciate it and became even more possessive of his "space" as he liked to call it.'

'How do you get on with him?'

'Surprisingly well. I put it that way because he is at daggers drawn with Amy. He obviously resents all the attention she gets here and since her illness he has had virtually nothing to do with her at all. To my great surprise, though, the Sunday before last he told my father something that may or may not have something to do with his murder. I think it best if he tells you what it was in his own words and I'll take you up there after we've had our coffee.

'As for Amy, there were problems at her boarding school two or three years ago and she was expelled for smoking cannabis and having sex with one of the boys there. My father was livid and told her that unless she got a grip on herself, she would ruin her life permanently. He arranged for her to be enrolled in a secretarial college in London for a year, then she got a job which she held down with very obvious lack of enthusiasm for eighteen months or so, but then she succumbed to ME. That was the last straw as far as Dad was concerned and he obviously decided to give up on her, leaving her management to her mother and the GP. That's how she got into the hands of the psychiatrists and all I can say about that is that it hasn't exactly proved to be a success. Here she is, a good year and a half later, no better at all and spends virtually all her time in bed, or sitting in the chair in her room.

'To be fair, it can't have been easy for Amy here. It is hardly surprising that she should have resented the attention my father paid to David and, in my opinion, that's one of the reasons why she developed ME. There were other factors as well; there had been the break-up of her natural parents' marriage and the problems I mentioned at her school. On my increasingly rare visits here, I found her to be both rude and surly but, to be fair, I didn't try as hard as I might have to get to know her after my initial overtures were ignored.'

'What's going to happen to David now?'

'He'll have to stay here for the time being and after that, I suppose it will depend on what comes out of all this. As Dad never formally adopted him, I suppose Jean's first husband must have some responsibility for him and I can't see Jean coping with an adolescent boy whom she neither understands, nor even likes. I expect him to get a university place and if he does, I hope that that will lead to his independence. My mother left all her money to me when she died and I fully agreed with Dad that he should draw up a new will when he remarried, leaving me out of it, apart from the contents of his study. He had a lot of books in there, many, but not all medical, reprints of his articles and memorabilia and photographs of our family before he married Jean. I don't know any more details about it than that, in particular what arrangements he made for Amy and David. He may, of course, have left everything to Jean or possibly made provision for them in the form of a trust. Apart from that, she'll no doubt get the house, the rest of the contents and half Dad's NHS pension and I also believe that she obtained a good divorce settlement from her first husband. I must say this for Jean, she's not a mercenary or particularly extravagant person and I don't anticipate any great problems.'

'I'm afraid that you won't be able to go into your father's study; we are going to seal it until our man has finished in there.'

'I expected that, but obviously I don't want Jean or anyone else in the house ferreting around in there, either.'

'I don't think you need worry about that. Would you let us have your address and phone numbers? We may need to contact you again in the next few days.'

'Of course.' She took a note pad out of her handbag and wrote them down, tore off the top piece of paper and handed it across. 'I've got some compassionate leave for the next few days and I will be available if you need me.'

'You do understand that there's bound to be an inquest and that our enquiries are bound to take some time.'

'Yes, of course.'

At that moment, the au pair girl came in with the tray on which was a cafetière, a jug of cream, three cups and saucers and a plate of biscuits. The young woman was strikingly pretty, dark-skinned, with glistening black hair and twinkling brown eyes. Interesting things were happening under her white shirt as she leaned over the table to pour Sarah's coffee and when his colleague looked up at her, Sinclair saw the girl's eyebrows rise up slightly. So that's the lie of the land, he thought. Initially, Sinclair wondered if Sarah had failed to notice it, but then she caught his eye and the slight flush on her cheeks indicated very clearly that she had.

'What about the accommodation down here?'

'I'll show it to you after we've finished our coffee. There are three large rooms, the sitting-room, the dining-room and Dad's study as well as the kitchen and a cloakroom on this floor.'

Before taking them upstairs, Rebecca Cochrane first showed them the dining-room. It was on the road side of the house and had a large circular table with eight chairs around it, a grandfather clock in one corner and a table with a variety of china and silver ornaments on it. The kitchen was also at the front on the other side of the substantial hall, on one side of which was the cloakroom and the staircase wound up from the other. The door of Cochrane's study had already been sealed by the scene-of-crime people.

'Who does the cooking?' Sarah asked.

'Jean, when she's in the mood, which is not very often. Mostly they live on ready meals and occasionally Monique does something for them. At one time, they used to give proper dinner parties, in which case they would get a caterer to come in.'

'What about the invalid?'

'She's a vegetarian and no wonder she looks half-starved, as most of the stuff Jean gets for her is taken off the shelves of the supermarket and heated up in the microwave. She does at least get plenty of fruit.'

'How does Mrs Cochrane occupy herself?'

'Certainly not by doing any housework or gardening. Her cleaning woman comes in every day except at the weekends and she spends a lot of her time at her club, which is only about a mile away. She plays bridge there, gossips with her friends and has the occasional game of tennis in the summer.'

'What about your father?'

'I gather that you already know about his study. It faces the back garden and that's where he used to write his medical papers, keep up to date by reading the psychiatric journals and he also had an electronic piano in there, usually playing it with earphones. Jean objected to him using the grand in the drawing-room, because the noise, as she put it, upset Amy.'

The young woman raised her eyebrows. 'In fact, he was rather good and used to perform regularly in the concerts organized by the staff at the hospital.

'Dad was very particular about that study. He kept it locked at all times, even when he was in there by himself, and wouldn't let anyone else to go into it, not even me or the cleaning woman. I don't know where the key is.'

'He was obviously very concerned about keeping that room private. Why do you suppose that was?' Sinclair asked.

'I imagine it must have been to stop Jean or anyone else from marching in and asking him stupid and unnecessary questions when he was working.' The young woman raised her eyebrows slightly. 'Anyway, Dad was like that, having a bit of an obsession about security. I only discovered that he liked to keep the gate between the garage and the house bolted on the inside at night when I was collecting him for a visit to Dr Paterson and his family early one Saturday morning. Rather than ring the front door bell, which is very loud and would have disturbed everyone, I tried to get in through the gate with a view to knocking on the kitchen door, but I found it had been secured on the inside. Dad must have seen my car from one of the upstairs windows because just as I was turning back to ring on the front door bell, he opened the gate and came hurrying out. He told me that, apart from the bell, as the front door of the house made quite a noise when one shut it, he always went out through the kitchen and into the garage through its rear door to get his car out for his journeys to the hospital early on weekday mornings. It was after that

that he gave me a spare electronic pad for opening the garage and a key for the door at the back of it, to allow me access to the pool without going through the house when they were away.

'Right, shall we go up to see David now? By the way, he always called Dad, James.'

CHAPTER THREE

Rebecca Cochrane took them up the stairs and knocked on the door of one of the bedrooms on the road side of the house.

'May I introduce Inspectors Prescott and Sinclair?' she said to the boy who had half-risen from his chair in front of the desk as they entered. 'They are looking into my dad's death and I thought it best for you to tell them what you discovered about Amy. Don't be embarrassed; this is very important so tell them in your words exactly what happened.'

The boy blinked at them from behind his thick glasses and then nodded. 'It was the Saturday of the week before last when James was away at a conference. I woke up in the night with a bit of a stomach ache and couldn't get back to sleep. I remember tossing and turning and it was then that I heard someone going down the stairs – they do creak a bit. I glanced at the luminous dial of my clock and saw that it was a few minutes after midnight.

'I didn't take much notice of it, thinking that perhaps Jean couldn't get to sleep and was going into the kitchen for something to eat, but then I heard the front door squeaking and so I got up and looked out through the gap in the curtains and saw someone hurrying along the path towards the road.'

'Who did you think it was?'

'Apart from me, there were only three others in the house; Jean always walks rather slowly, Monique's hair is too dark and she is too tall for the person I saw, and so it had to be Amy.'

'Did you see if she met anyone?' Sarah asked.

'No, but I did hear a car start up soon after. It was some way off and didn't make much noise, but by that time I had opened the window.'

'What did you do next?'

'I still had a stomach ache and tried to get back to sleep, but it didn't work and at about five I decided to get up and finish some schoolwork on my computer rather than toss and turn in bed. It was beginning to get light when I heard a car again and this time I saw Amy clearly enough to be sure it was her.'

'Did you have any suspicion prior to that that Amy wasn't really ill?'

'I knew that James didn't believe so; he and Jean once had a serious row about it and I asked Rebecca about it. She explained that some people, like my father, felt that a bit like anorexia nervosa, ME had no detectable cause and giving it a name, which implied that it was some sort of infection, was not helpful in getting to the bottom of the condition.'

'If you were right that it was Amy, why do you suppose she was behaving in this way?'

'I don't know. Anyway, directly James got back on the Sunday afternoon, I told him what I had heard and seen.'

'How did he react?'

'He thanked me and said I had done the right thing, but not to tell anyone else about it until he had had a chance to think about it. I kept my word, but after James's death, I thought Rebecca ought to know about it.'

'What about the doctor from the hospital who came to see Amy regularly? Did you ever meet him?'

'I let him in a couple of times when I was here during the school holidays and he seemed very nice. He chatted to me for a few minutes and I remember he asked me about school and the subjects I was doing. He was also very interested when I told him about my train set in the loft and asked if I would show it to him. He wasn't just saying that, either; I gave him a demonstration and he was very enthusiastic about it. He told me that he had had a set-up when he was a boy, but it was nothing like as good as mine.'

'Did you mention anything about Amy being out at night to your mother after Dr Cochrane was killed?'

'I asked Rebecca about that and she said that it was better not to do so, at least until after she had had a word with the police.'

Sinclair turned towards Rebecca Cochrane. 'Have you mentioned any of this to Mrs Cochrane yourself?'

'No; as David said, I thought it best not to as she was in such an emotional state and I didn't want to add to her distress.'

Sinclair nodded. 'Are you convinced, yourself, that it was Amy?'

'I don't see who else it could have been. After all, David knows her very well and the only other person it might have been is Monique and as David pointed out to me, she has black hair, whereas Amy's is blonde, and she is much taller and quicker in her movements.'

'Well, thank you, David,' Sinclair said, 'that was very helpful.'

'What's going to happen now?' the boy asked.

'We will need to search the house very thoroughly, which means, I'm afraid, that it may be necessary for everyone to move out to a hotel. If it has to be done, and I'll need to discuss it with the Chief Superintendent who is in charge of the investigation beforehand, it shouldn't be for very long.'

The boy stood there staring at the detective unblinkingly and Rebecca Cochrane turned towards him and smiled. 'Don't worry, David, I'll just introduce the detectives to Jean and then I'll come back and have another chat with you. All right?'

The boy nodded, but didn't say anything back, just looked straight at her.

'There's one thing you should know before you see Jean and Amy,' Rebecca said, as they stood on the landing after leaving the boy's room. 'On the Monday after dad got back from his conference, he rang me up and told me what David has said about Amy and that he had taken a sample of her blood. He then asked me if I would arrange for it to be tested at my hospital, St Gregory's.'

'And it proved positive for drugs?' Sarah asked.

'Yes, cocaine and alcohol.'

'Right. Thank you. You haven't told anyone else about this, have you?'

'No, I haven't.'

'Good. We'd like you to keep it under wraps for the time being. I take it that you didn't give Amy's name to your lab.'

'No. I made up a story to a friend of mine, who works in pathology and to whom I gave the specimen, and she promised to analyse it herself on the q.t.'

'Good.'

'You might like to see Jean in her bedroom,' Rebecca said. 'If I know her, it'll be ages before she is ready to come down.'

'Perhaps I'll have a chat to her on my own to start with,' Sarah said. 'If she is in an anxious state, let alone not fully dressed, she might feel more relaxed with just me and after that maybe she'll take me in to see Amy. Meanwhile, Inspector Sinclair will have a word with Monique; he speaks French fluently.'

'That makes good sense to me. By the way, while I'm on leave I plan to see Dad's solicitor. I am an executor of his will and later on, when you've finished here, I'd like to make a start on sorting out his books and the reprints of the articles he has published, which I would like to keep, and I want to make sure that Jean doesn't get her sticky fingers on them and throw them out.'

'I'm sure that there'll be no difficulty with that, but I know you understand that you won't be able to make a start for some time. There will also have to be an inquest first,' Sinclair said.

'Yes, I do realize all that. Excuse me a moment, I'll just go up and see how Jean's getting on.'

The young woman came back almost straight away. 'Madame is just about to raise enough energy to get into her bath, so perhaps seeing Amy first would be a better bet. Before I go, I think I ought to take you into her room and introduce you to her, otherwise she might get into a panic. It's not up to me, of course, but may I suggest that Inspector Prescott sees Amy on her own in the first instance. She's in rather a fragile state this morning.' Rebecca Cochrane raised her eyebrows slightly. 'After that, I'll have another quick word with David and then I'll be off.'

'Right,' said Sinclair, 'all that makes good sense. Thank you for all your help.'

'It was the least I could do.'

With a brief nod in Sinclair's direction she turned away and walked briskly towards Amy's room, with Sarah following behind.

Sinclair stood for several minutes on the landing, looking out of the window deep in thought, and was just starting to make his way down the stairs in order to see the au pair girl, when Rebecca Cochrane came hurrying out of David's room.

'I'm glad I caught you. David's gone completely to pieces now that he knows about the hotel, but he managed to keep it to himself until I got back just now. He's worried about his schoolwork with the exams coming up and he can't bear the thought of being in the same place as Amy, whom he thinks has been responsible for everything that has gone wrong. She's a cheat and a liar, he said, and he knew, he just knew, that Jean would be on her side. I am only too familiar with David's moods by now, but I've never known him like this before. He asked me if he could stay with me until everything had settled down. He promised me that he wouldn't be a nuisance, that he'd get his own breakfast, that he'd be at school all day and he'd have lots of revision to do in the evenings.'

'What's your own view about that?'

'I can't say that I'm absolutely enchanted by the idea and it would be quite impossible when I get back to work, but I reckon I could cope with him until the end of the exams next Friday.'

'Won't that be very inconvenient for you?'

'It's not as if David would be hanging about all day. All I'll need to do is take him to school in the car and collect him in the afternoon. Apart from that, it'll just be a question of an evening meal and seeing that he gets to bed at a reasonable hour.

'I understand just how difficult it would be for him to face Amy now that he knows that she isn't and hasn't really been ill. It was one thing when she was shut up in her room and had Monique to look after her and Dr Clarke visiting regularly, but not now. Jean could never keep a secret and I agree with him that Amy is bound to find out that it was he who had told my father about seeing her leaving the house in the small hours of that Saturday night. David clearly thinks that he would be in serious danger from her and he told me that he was desperately worried and that she might even think of killing him.

'I told him that that idea was way over the top and did my best to calm him down, but I could see at once that it wasn't going to work.'

'How would Jean take to that suggestion, do you suppose?'

'I know that the two of them haven't been getting on for some time and I think she would be relieved, although you can be sure that she won't show it. I'm quite prepared to tackle her myself, so why don't I do that now, while Inspector Prescott's with Amy? I've only got to flatter her a bit, by saying that her hands will be full with Amy and that she's the only person able to look after her now that all this has blown up. She may put up a token resistance, but she'll go along with it, I know she will.'

Sinclair nodded. 'I don't see why you shouldn't do that, if you're sure you're up to it. However, David won't be able to take his laptop with him. I'm not implying anything by that, but I'm sure you appreciate that we can't afford to leave anything to chance.'

'But what about his schoolwork?'

'One of our computer and electronic experts is already here and he'll be able to put anything David needs from his laptop on to a CD, which will no doubt be readable on your own system, which I'm sure you'd let David use.'

The young woman nodded. 'I don't have any problem with that and I'll be around to supervise him. Might I suggest that I take him back to my flat with me later this morning. Like a lot of obsessionals, he gets distinctly twitchy if things are not cut and dried. Jean is the complete opposite of that – she's absolutely chaotic where arrangements are concerned and the two of them get on each other's nerves as it is. When would your technician be able to do what you suggest?'

'I'll have a word with him right now and he should be able to come up to David's room straight away.'

'David's bound to ask me why you want his laptop. Is there any particular reason?'

'No, just routine in a case like this and we'll be doing the same with your father's and any others that might be here. When I've seen Mr Pocock, I'll wait here for Inspector Prescott until she's finished with Amy, so that I'll be able to tell her what's going on and she'll be forewarned that Jean Cochrane's quite likely to be upset.'

Sinclair decided to wait until Rebecca and David had left the house and Sarah was with Jean Cochrane in the woman's bedroom before going to see the au pair girl. She was in the kitchen and smiled and raised her eyebrows when he spoke to her in French.

'I'd like a word with you and as it's such a lovely morning,' he said, 'why don't we go out into the garden? Perhaps there's somewhere out there where we won't be disturbed.'

'There's a seat by the side of the swimming pool.'

'Yes, I saw it when we went out to the summerhouse. I

understand that Dr Cochrane used to work on his designs in there.'

'Yes, mostly at the weekends. He showed some of them to me once and they were really good, very detailed and colourful.'

'How long have you been here?' Sinclair asked, when they were seated by the pool.

'Nearly a year.'

'And do you like it?'

'Sometimes it's very good and sometimes not so good.'

The detective smiled. 'Tell me about the good bits first.'

'It is a really nice part of London here and soon after I arrived Dr Cochrane introduced me to a lovely family who live up the road. Their daughter, Jess, is about my age and is having a gap year after leaving school before going to university. She's going to study modern languages there and Dr Cochrane thought that it would help my English and her French if we got on well together.'

'And you do?'

'Oh, yes. We go riding in the park and she comes to swim here. She is lovely and her family are very nice. We also go to central London sometimes on my day off.'

'Does anyone else use the pool?'

'Dr Cochrane's daughter, Rebecca, whom you've just met, did sometimes when she came out for lunch on Sundays when he was working in the summerhouse. That's the day when I sometimes cook the meal.'

'Did you like Dr Cochrane?'

'Oh, yes. He was always so nice to me. He used to chat to me, helped me with my English and was very interested in news of my family. You see, when he was seventeen he stayed with them in Sarlat. My grandfather had been with De Gaulle in England during the war and that's where he met Dr Cochrane's father. They kept in touch; my father came over here to visit the Cochrane family and in return Dr Cochrane stayed with ours for a month one summer. When I thought of working in London as an au pair, my father told me about Dr Cochrane, got in touch with him and so that's why I am here. He was quite happy to have me as a guest, but my mother thought that a year would be far too long and it would be best for me to come as an au pair. He was very good to me about that, too, making sure that I had enough time off.'

'How do you get on with Mrs Cochrane?'

The young woman smiled. 'She is not a nice woman, but she has to be careful with me, because she knows I wouldn't stay if she treated me like she did her husband. I don't know why he let her get away with it; she was always shouting at him and telling him to do things she could easily do herself.'

'Is she the same with Rebecca?'

The young woman raised her eyebrows. 'Rebecca frightens her, I think. She is very direct, quite unlike her father. I remember once, when the family were all sitting near the summerhouse after Sunday lunch, Jean told her to fetch her cardigan from the sitting room as she was cold, without so much as a please, just the way she used to speak to her husband. Rebecca just stared at her and said, "I'm here as my father's guest, Jean, not as your servant. I suggest you get it yourself." I don't suppose she had ever been spoken to like that before.'

'How did she react to that?'

'She flushed, looked at her husband, then at me, seemed about to say something, then changed her mind as Rebecca continued to stare at her.'

'How about Dr Cochrane?'

'He didn't say anything, just looked at the ground. I could see how embarrassed he was, but I knew he wouldn't tell Rebecca off.'

'How did you know that?'

'It's difficult to explain; she has that effect on people.'

'What happened next?'

'I don't know. I thought it best to load up the tray and take it back to the kitchen.'

'Did Mrs Cochrane behave to other men in the same way as she did to her husband?'

The young woman smiled. 'Oh, no. You should see the way she is with the doctor who comes to see Amy. He is very handsome and flatters her, saying things such as, "You look far too young to be Amy's mother."'

'How does she react to that?'

'She clearly loves it and goes all girly. He always goes to talk to her in her room after he has seen Amy to "report progress" as he says.'

The young woman raised her eyebrows and smiled.

'Do you mean that he does rather more with her than just discussing Amy?'

'I have heard some strange noises coming from her bedroom several times when he was in there.' The girl raised her eyebrows slightly. 'My mother sometimes gave me a sound spanking when I was very naughty as a child and once it sounded rather like that.'

'Is that all he did with Mrs Cochrane?'

'No. I'm sure they went all the way as well.'

'Did Dr Clarke ever try it on with you?'

'No. He obviously knows a lot about sex, you see, and realizes that I am not interested in men in that way.'

'How does he behave with Amy?'

'He is always very correct. He always insists on my being there when he is with her and if he examines her it is always done with great delicacy. Anyway, Amy pretends to be very shy about her body and even tried it on with me. I wouldn't have it and told her that if she was that sensitive and didn't want me to help her get in and out of the bath, she could do it herself.'

'How do you get on with her?'

'All right, but no more than that. She sleeps a lot and doesn't say much to me.'

'Do you think she really is ill?'

'Oh, yes. Why else would someone of her age stay in one room most of the time? She would be quite pretty if she put on some weight and had some colour in her cheeks.'

'Did she have any visitors?'

'Just a young man of about her own age; Amy told me that he had been at school with her and that he was a bore. Dr Cochrane, though, seemed to like him a lot. He used to take her for drives when he came here on Sundays and was always very polite and well-dressed and always brought Amy back punctually. I heard Dr Cochrane talking about him to his wife and saying that getting out in the fresh air and a change of scene was just what Amy needed and that it was such a pity that she didn't seem to like the young man all that much. That wasn't the half of it; Amy told me once that he was drag, a do-gooder and always trying to convert her and saying that if she prayed to God together with him, he was sure she would get better. That wasn't Amy's scene at all, but I don't think she knew how to get rid of him, particularly as Dr Cochrane and her mother were always singing his praises.'

'So Amy didn't enjoy his visits?'

'No, she told me more than once that she dreaded them.'

'Did you meet him?'

'Yes, most of the times he came. I used to help him get Amy into the car.'

'What was he like?'

'Very good-looking and obviously very rich, with a fancy car and expensive clothes. I could see what Amy meant, though; he was not the sort of person with whom one could have fun and a bit of a laugh. Dr Cochrane, though, was most impressed and I heard him say once to his wife that if only she could settle down with someone like him, it would be the making of her.'

'Do you think that getting out of the house was doing her good?'

'No, I don't. When she came back, she always looked terribly tired and usually had a long sleep afterwards.'

'Do you know if she ever had a boyfriend apart from him?'

'No, I don't and it's not as if he was a proper one, either. I overheard him say to Mrs Cochrane that he felt sorry for Amy, that it was his Christian duty to try to help her and that he hoped that his visits might cheer her up.'

'Did she ever go out with anyone else while you've been here?'

The girl grinned at him. 'No, but my friend Jess told me that her brother took her out once just before she got ill, but it didn't work out and he never tried again. They just weren't on the same wavelength.'

'Have you met your friend's brother yourself?'

'Oh, yes. He still lives at home. He's very charming and good-looking and could have any girl he wanted, but Jess says he's only interested in making money, tinkering with his Porsche and playing polo. He works for a promotions company in London. He's good fun and I like him a lot.'

'How does Mrs Cochrane treat Amy?'

'As if she was a baby. She is always stroking her cheeks and crying over her.'

'What about Dr Cochrane?'

'He was obviously worried about her, but although he tried to hide it, I think he was also irritated by her, clearly thinking that she wasn't making any effort. I saw him once shaking his head as he came out of her room and Amy and her mother obviously thought he was unsympathetic. He believed that lying in bed for most of the day and not making any real effort was the worst thing possible for her. It got so bad that she didn't want to see him at all and I was very surprised when he came on the Sunday evening before last with a syringe and told her that the lady doctor at the hospital wanted him to take a blood sample for some new test.'

'And she agreed to let him do it?'

'I don't think she wanted to, but he said that Dr Clarke wasn't available that day and that Dr Clements wanted the specimen as soon as possible. He told her that the alternative would be for an ambulance to take her to the hospital and that would be selfish of her and quite unacceptable. He was very direct and masterful with her and she gave way.'

'Were you present when he took the blood?'

'Oh, yes. He insisted on it.'

'And did she make a fuss?'

'No. He was very stern with her and I think she was quite shaken. You see, she was used to her mother speaking to her as if she was a baby and always getting her own way.'

'How do you get on with David?

'David is not a nice boy. He is always creeping around, never saying anything much, and once Jess told me that she was sure that he was spying on us while we were sunbathing. I don't think he did it again after we caught him at it, though.'

'How did you manage that?'

'We saw some movement in the bushes opposite the pool

and Jess suggested that I put on a show, while she pretended to go back to the house for some suncream. It worked brilliantly. She walked off and while I fooled about topless, doing a few cartwheels and handstands, she circled round and came up behind where he was hiding. Jess is a big strong girl and got hold of his hair, dragged him to the edge of the pool and threw him in. David can't swim and after letting him struggle for a minute or two, she jumped in herself, pulled him along to the shallow end and when she had lifted him out, told him that if he ever tried it on with us again, she'd tell Dr Cochrane. She would have done so, too.'

Sinclair raised his eyebrows. 'When was all that?'

'About three weeks ago.'

'Do you think he got the message?'

'I'm sure he did. He's avoided us both ever since.'

'Are you going to stay on here in view of what's happened to Dr Cochrane?'

'I will at least until my friend goes to university in the autumn and perhaps I'll leave after that.'

Sinclair nodded. 'I think it's time I went back to the house; I'm very grateful for your help. I'll wait for my colleague in the drawing-room.'

The girl smiled. 'It was nice to use my own language again. I've often heard people say that the English can't speak foreign languages – they were wrong.'

'You flatter me.'

*

Sinclair had plenty of time during which to ponder on what he had heard from the young woman, as Sarah did not reappear for another twenty minutes.

'Sorry to have kept you,' she said, 'but the situation regarding Jean Cochrane was a bit tricky, to say the least of it.'

'That I can well believe. How did you get on?'

'I'll deal with Amy first. The girl obviously wasn't too keen on being seen alone and asked Rebecca if she or her mother could be there with her. As you may imagine, Rebecca brushed that aside and told her not to be such a baby, saying that she had too much to do and that her mother wasn't fully dressed. All that rather took the wind out of her sails and, although she was undoubtedly anxious, she didn't refuse to cooperate.

'Anyway, if what is implied by David is true and Amy is making her illness up, she is quite some actress. She is as pale as a ghost, speaks with a soft "little girl" voice and looks at one with doe eyes.

'I asked her if her illness was getting her down and she gave me a sad little smile and said, "I try not to let it do so and Dr Clarke is very kind to me and says that it will get better in time and that it is very important that I believe that. He is such a nice man, very correct and the sort of person to give one confidence. He never sees me entirely on his own and always insists that either my mother or Monique is there as well. I can understand why he does that when he examines me, but I would quite like to speak to him in private some times. However, as he explained, Dr Clements is in charge of my case and the time to ask any questions that are worrying me is when I see her on my own at the hospital. In that way, he said, I won't get mixed messages, which could so easily lead to misunderstandings. My mother also says that he always takes the trouble to see her after he has left me, reassures her and answers questions patiently.

'I asked her how her mother had reacted to her illness and she said, "That is the thing that worries me more than anything else. She is so concerned about me that I sometimes think that she might be going to have a nervous breakdown." As for James, she told me she found it hurtful that he thought she was just neurotic and hysterical, although she had to admit that he never actually said that to her face. She said she felt sorry for him, Dr Clarke having told her that there had been unpleasantness between him and Dr Clements over the subject of ME as a whole and that there were rumours that he was contemplating legal action over an article she had written.

'She also said that she was really surprised when Cochrane came to take a sample of blood from her and he explained that by saying that he had heard about a new test for ME at the conference he had attended during the previous two days and that although it wasn't always positive in the condition, Dr Clements wanted to carry it out on as many sufferers from it as possible. Evidently she asked him why Dr Clarke couldn't take it as he was due to see her only three days later.'

'And what was his answer?'

'That Dr Clements was doing the research on ME and wanted as few people as possible to know about it before it was published. Amy thought that there must have been some sort of rapprochement between the two of them and decided not to mention it to Dr Clarke, but he noticed the puncture mark and small bruise at the bend of her elbow, asked her about it and she felt she had to tell him exactly what Cochrane had said.'

'Did she say how Clarke reacted?'

'Apparently he just nodded and then carried on with her usual regimen of exercises.'

'Did she say anything about Dr Clements?'

'Just that she wasn't friendly like Dr Clarke and never seemed to smile. I got the impression that she was scared of the woman.'

'So what did you finally make of her after all that?'

Sarah thought for a moment. 'Had I not known what David said, I have to say I would have thought that she was totally convincing. Everything she said was reasonable, she looks washed out and unwell and she didn't make any attempt to run her stepfather down. The results of the blood test, though, are clearly crucial and it seems to me likely that Cochrane was intending to have the sample analyzed somewhere away from Henshaw Hospital and hadn't got round to it and just left it in the summerhouse.'

'Rebecca explained that to me. Evidently, Cochrane gave her one of the specimens and asked her to have it analyzed at her hospital. I think it likely that he kept the second sample as a back-up, and no doubt Tredgold will be able to confirm that. And what was your impression of Mrs Cochrane?'

'She was obviously put out of countenance by Rebecca, who took me in to see her and explained what she planned to do with David. However, I think that she was extremely relieved not to have to deal with him as well as the possible move to a hotel. However, once Rebecca had gone, she soon settled down and played "The Tragedy Queen". Her husband was dead, her daughter very ill and David would hardly ever say anything to her. What was she going to do? I felt a strong impulse to tell her to pull herself together and take charge of everything, but of course I didn't. In effect, she didn't really answer any of my questions properly. She implied that she had loved her husband dearly, but that her daughter's illness had come between them. That David was withdrawn and never spoke to her and that Rebecca was ignoring her and taking over.

'Put like that it may not sound unreasonable, but it was all said with great dramatic effect and I was left doubting if she meant any of it.'

'Would it interest you to know,' Sinclair said, raising his eyebrows, 'that Monique told me that after seeing Amy, Clarke was in the habit of going to Mrs Cochrane's bedroom and banging her?'

'What?'

'Part of the entertainment for the young woman was to listen outside her door when she discovered that he liked *lutiner les femmes* and on one occasion she even heard the woman being on the receiving end of what she thought was *une bonne fessée*.'

'Are those things as bad as they sound?'

'I came across the former when I was reading a biography, written in French, of Rasputin. Apparently the notorious monk liked "a bit of slap and tickle" with the ladies and sometimes rather more than that. As to the latter, it means a sound spanking.'

Sarah laughed. 'Show-off. I can think of others who have the same urges.'

'What about those who enjoy being on the receiving end?'

'Enough said. Did you believe Monique?'

'Yes, I did. She was also at pains to point out, as I had suspected already, that she was gay and had a great friendship with the daughter of the house a couple of hundred yards up the road, a student on her gap year before going to university. That was the main reason why she had stayed in England. She had found Mrs Cochrane a major pain right from the start, although she liked and respected her husband, who made a point of chatting to her whenever the opportunity arose.'

'The plot certainly thickens. What do you suppose the General Medical Council would think of Clarke's behaviour?' Sarah asked.

'Hardly approval, but Mrs Cochrane isn't Clarke's patient and I think it unlikely that they would do anything more than censure him. I have little doubt, though, that if it came out, his future at Henshaw Hospital would be problematic in the extreme. What do you suggest for this afternoon?'

'We'll clearly have to sort out the removal of the three women from here as quickly as possible, but that won't be possible until we see Tyrrell tomorrow when he'll have to make the decision about their departure. Rebecca having taken David off to her flat will make it both easier and cheaper,' Sarah said.

Sinclair nodded. 'I'd like to make my number with Mrs Cochrane and put the best possible spin I can on David's departure and warn her of the likelihood that she, Amy and the au pair will almost certainly have to leave the house for a few days and in the very near future at that. How do you think she'll take it?'

'Outrage followed by relief would be my guess,' Sarah said, 'and after that, I thought that perhaps a word with Monique's friend up the road might be worthwhile. There's no point in hanging around here while Jack and his team are still beavering away.'

'In that case, why don't we find a pub somewhere to get our strength back? Monique might know of one not too far away.'

The French girl was preparing a salad to go with a substantial amount of smoked salmon, which was already laid out on a plate with thin slices of brown bread and butter.

'Why not have some of this and some fruit?' she said in response to Sinclair's question about a pub. 'I was expecting Rebecca and David to be here, but now that they've gone, there'll be plenty to go round. I'll bring it to you in the sitting-room, if you like.'

Sinclair looked at Sarah and raised his eyebrows slightly. 'That's not a bad idea. What do you think?'

'I agree.' She turned towards the French girl and smiled at

her. 'Thank you, Monique, that would be lovely. Perhaps Mrs Cochrane might join us. My colleague would like to meet her.'

The young woman looked across at Sinclair and said something to him in rapid French.

'*D'accord*,' he replied, nodding and smiling at her. 'Oh, by the way,' he said, continuing in French, 'our people will be here for most of the afternoon, looking at Dr Cochrane's study and bedroom, but they shouldn't need to disturb you. We will probably have departed before they have finished and they will lock up and tape Dr Cochrane's study, his bedroom and the summerhouse before they go and it's almost certain that they'll want to come back again tomorrow and for the next day or two.'

'What was all that about?' Sarah said when the young woman had gone.

'I was just explaining about Jack Pocock and his team and warned her about the possibility of a move to a hotel. She also told me she'd put a large bomb under 'er upstairs, but doesn't hold out too much hope of her appearing all that soon.'

Sinclair had been wondering what a man like the senior registrar, Andrew Clarke, could possibly see in a married woman, the wife of a senior colleague of his, and more than that, the mother of a patient. He changed his mind directly he saw Jean Cochrane. She had obviously taken a great deal of trouble over her appearance, her hair and make-up being immaculate. She was wearing a simple cotton dress and as she turned towards the easy chair after shaking hands, Sarah saw him glance at her firm backside and, catching his eye, gave him the suspicion of a wink.

'I'm sorry that we have had to disturb you at such a sad a time as this,' he said, 'but I'm sure you understand that we have to look very carefully into all the circumstances concerning your husband's death. A search warrant has already been obtained, as no doubt you've been told, but we will probably have to ask all of you to leave the house in order to carry out our investigations as thoroughly as possible. It seems very likely that you will have to move out for a few days very soon, although a final decision has yet to be taken. We will make sure that you are taken to a good hotel, as close to here as possible.'

The woman dabbed the corner of her eye with her handkerchief and nodded. 'Of course, you must do what you have to, but I would ask you to handle Amy as carefully as you are able. She is very fragile, you know, and it is a relief to me not to have to worry about David just at the moment. He is at a difficult age just now and with his exams coming up....' Her voice trailed off and she let out a deep sigh. 'Who could have done such a terrible thing to James?'

'That's what we are doing our utmost to find out,' Sinclair said. 'Did your husband ever mention any problems he might have been having here or at the hospital?'

'Well, there was, of course, Amy's illness, which, it has to be said, has disrupted our lives in so many ways and the dispute James was having with one of his colleagues over its nature.'

'Did he explain to you what that was about?'

'I think it would have been so much better if he had. It was Dr Clarke who told me about it. He is so sympathetic, takes so much trouble over Amy and she has real confidence in him. He is quite unlike that severe woman at the hospital; I have only met her once at the initial consultation and I didn't take to her at all.

'I know that Amy feels the same way about Dr Clarke as I do. He is very correct and always likes to have another person of the same gender there as well whenever he examines her. He explained that young women like Amy usually feel more comfortable if they have another woman there to support them under those circumstances. Amy found that very reassuring as she has always been shy about her body and I'll always be grateful to Monique for being with her during his visits. I know that Amy would have liked to talk to him on her own, but he told her that Dr Clements wouldn't approve as it was important that she didn't get mixed messages about her illness.'

'Did your husband seem in any way different in the days before he died?' Sinclair asked.

'If anything, he appeared rather more relaxed than usual and was very pleased with the way the conference had gone, with several interesting new ideas being discussed.'

'I realize that quite a few married couples have separate bedrooms for all sorts of reasons and I wonder why that was so in your case,' Sarah asked.

The woman didn't appear to be in the least put out by the question.

'James was very considerate like that. He was often restless at night, waking and not being able to get off to sleep again and sometimes would go down to his study to read for a bit or play something on his electronic piano with the earphones on. He also liked to leave for work very early. He appreciated that I wasn't an early morning person and never expected me or Monique to get his breakfast.'

'How about David? Did he get his own, too?'

'He only ever had cereal, fruit, toast and marmalade, with orange juice to drink and also liked to get it himself.'

'How did he get to and back from school?' Sinclair asked.

'If it was fine he went on his bicycle and if wet, I used to take him in my car.'

'How do you think David is going to take all this?' Sarah asked.

'David has been a great worry to me for a long time. He keeps himself very much to himself and when he's not at school, he's either in his room studying or up in the loft playing with his trains. James always tried to reassure me by saying that it was just a phase and that a lot of boys of his age were like that. Rebecca told me that David was very upset this morning, that he was worried about the effects all the upheaval would have on his work for the exams and begged her to let him stay with her for a few days.'

'What is your view about that?'

'It's no secret that at times I find Rebecca overbearing and managing and have often wondered if she has any feelings inside her at all. Her behaviour this morning is typical; she just blew in and took charge. Having said that, though, I'm very grateful to her for taking care of David at this difficult time. I've got enough on my plate with having to look after Amy as well as cope with my utter devastation and grief.'

'Well, thank you for your help,' Sinclair said. 'We won't need to disturb you again this afternoon. One of our men and his assistants are looking at the summerhouse and Dr Cochrane's study and bedroom and may take some time. I'm sure that they won't disturb you and will let themselves out when they have finished. They will be sealing all three places and coming to have a look at the rest of the house over the next few days, but let me assure you that this is just routine and nothing for you to worry about. We will, of course, be in touch with you later if there are any new developments.'

After the woman had gone, saying that she had a lot of letters to write in response to the many she had already received, Sinclair gave Sarah a quizzical look.

'That was a big surprise,' he said. 'I was expecting more than a touch of the tragedy queen.'

Sarah nodded, deciding to keep the fact that she was quite sure that Jean Cochrane had found Mark more than a little attractive very much to herself. 'So was I,' she said.

After the two detectives had had a word with Pocock, Sinclair found the French girl in the kitchen.

'We are very grateful for all the help you have given us,' he said, 'and if there are any problems or developments you think we should know about, please don't hesitate to get in touch with me by giving me a ring on my mobile phone. I've written down the number on my card here. There's no reason why you shouldn't use the swimming pool on your own or with your friend from now on, but the summerhouse will be secured. We would also like to talk briefly to your friend's parents about Dr Cochrane and perhaps you would let me know their telephone number. I'd like to give them at least some warning that we're coming.'

'Of course,' she said. 'Their name is Foster and they are all very nice. I'm sure they'll help you in any way they can.'

CHAPTER FOUR

THE FOSTERS' HOUSE was a hundred yards or so down the road and on the opposite side, and when they were just short of it they saw a young man bent forward and peering into the engine compartment at the rear of an old Porsche 911, which was standing in the drive in front of the double garage. He straightened up and turned round on hearing their approach.

'You must be the detectives,' he said with a smile. 'I'm Bob Foster and my mother told me to expect you.' He held up his hands, which were covered with grease. 'You won't thank me for shaking yours. Very sad about James Cochrane; thoroughly nice fellow.'

'Did you know him well?'

'No, but he always had a word if we met in the road and I showed him the car once and took him for a spin. My sister's the one who knew him best. You're probably aware that she is great friends with the Cochranes' au pair and he let them use the pool whenever it was free, which was most of the time. Otherwise, he and his daughter, Rebecca, were the only other ones to use it and that was not very often.'

'Did you know Amy at all?' Sarah asked.

'Funny girl. I took her to watch a polo match in which I was playing a year or two ago in Windsor Great Park, and it was a disaster. She didn't like the car, which got us off to a bad start and didn't actually endear her to me. She said it was smelly, noisy and uncomfortable. She also didn't like anything in the picnic which my mother had taken a lot of trouble over and, despite my warning, she wore a ridiculous pair of high-heeled shoes – hardly suitable for treading down divots.' The young man grinned at them. 'It was all my fault, really. I met her at a party at the Cochranes' place and should have realized that she wasn't my sort of girl. My sister told me I was an idiot to ask her out and she was right. Shame about her illness, though; I wouldn't wish that on anyone.'

'Does your sister know her well?'

The young man shook his head. 'Chalk and cheese. Jess is sports mad; riding, running and swimming are what she lives for and she's found just the right friend in Monique. Perhaps you've met her.'

'Yes, we have.'

'Then you'll know what I mean.' He raised his eyebrows and grinned at them.

'Having a week off, are you?' Sarah asked.

'Yes, there's an important polo match on Sunday next and I've been practising in the park; you may have seen the pitch, which is just inside the Roehampton Gate up the road. Why not give a ring on the front door bell? Mum's expecting you.'

Claire Foster was as direct and forceful as her son. 'I have to confess that the few times I met Jean Cochrane, I didn't take to her at all. It was as much my fault as hers. Gardening, riding and serious walking are as alien to her as fashion is to me. I liked James, though. He was such a nice man, always pausing for a word when I was working in the front garden and he was on his way to the post at the weekends. He was also very good to Jess, who has become very friendly with Monique, the Cochranes' au pair girl. The two of them get on really well and James allowed them to use his swimming pool whenever they liked, provided that they didn't disturb him when he was working in the summerhouse. You may not know that he was an expert calligrapher, and he took the trouble to show Jess some of his beautiful work and even let her try her hand at something simple. She has got really enthusiastic about it and has even joined a class in calligraphy at the local adult education centre during this, her gap year, and he was really encouraging about her early efforts.'

'We've met Monique,' Sinclair said. 'She obviously likes your daughter very much and, reading between the lines, we doubt if she would have stayed with the Cochranes had it not been for their friendship. She wasn't exactly complaining about Amy to us, but she clearly had to do a great deal for her, way beyond that usually expected of au pairs, as I understand it.'

'I couldn't agree more. Monique is a lovely girl, always cheerful and we all like her enormously. It's not only all the riding and swimming the two girls do together, either; between them they have had English and French days with enormous benefit to each other's languages.'

'Amy seems a very sad person,' Sarah said.

'It's a tragedy. Alec, my husband, thinks she needs a boot up the backside and cold baths twice a day, but that seems to me to be very harsh. I've read a certain amount about ME and who, at that age, would choose to take to their bed for a lot of the time for months or even years? It seems to me to have many parallels with anorexia nervosa.

'I'm afraid that Bob had no patience with her, either; I can't think why he ever asked her out in the first place. Even when she was well, she looked as if the first puff of wind would blow her over. As far as she was concerned, one might also ask why she ever agreed to go out with a polo player, of all people. I must say this for her, though, she didn't make the same mistake twice, nor did he for that matter.'

'Is your daughter, Jess, in?' Sarah asked. 'There have been suggestions that Dr Cochrane was depressed recently and, as she must have seen him quite often, we wondered if she had noticed anything.'

'She's working on a design in her room, but I'm sure she'd be happy to have a word with you.'

The young woman was a bit like her mother, being rather hearty and brimming with energy.

'I was so sorry to hear about Dr Cochrane,' she said. 'He was rather a serious man, but very nice in his way and always ready to have a chat and seemed genuinely interested in what I was doing. Have you seen any of his calligraphy?'

'Only the piece he was currently working on in the summer-house.'

'It's amazing, not only technically, but the designs on his cards and book plates were brilliant. He had a very good eye for fashion, too; I have flirted with it by sketching some of my attempts at fashion design and he made a lot of constructive suggestions about them.'

'Did he give you the impression of being anxious and depressed recently?' Sinclair asked.

'Worried, yes, but not depressed. You see, he was very concerned about Amy and was surprisingly forthcoming to me about her. He thought that the people looking after her were too passive in their management of her illness, just letting her moulder away a lot of the time in bed and that some fresh air and gradually building up a programme of exercise would be much better for her, not to mention improving her nutrition. Monique felt the same and, after all, she saw more of Amy than anyone else. I worry about Monique, too. Now that Dr Cochrane has gone, I think there is a real danger of her being exploited. He always checked to make sure that she was getting enough time off and now....' The young woman looked round to make sure that the door was fully closed. 'That stupid woman, Amy's mother, just wrings her hands and says that Monique is so good with Amy and that she would be lost without her. The result is that she does almost nothing for Amy herself. I can tell you this; if I had been in Monique's position, I wouldn't have let her get away it. Anyway, if at any time Monique's had enough, she could always come and stay here; we've got a spare room and Mum could do with a bit of help.'

'What about Rebecca? Do you know her?' Sarah asked.

'I've only met her a couple of times, but it's obvious that she's as hard as nails with none of her father's charm. I think Mrs Cochrane's terrified of her.'

'Have you met the doctor who comes from the hospital to see Amy?'

'No, but Monique has told me about him.' The young woman raised her eyebrows 'I'd better not say in what way, but I gather that he manages Mrs Cochrane rather well.'

'I gathered from your mother that Amy's visit to the polo match with your brother was not exactly a success.'

Jess Foster let out a hoot of laughter. 'She was wearing the most ridiculous shoes with high heels and I just knew what was going to happen, not least because the ground was quite soft. They were sucked off her and that was the end of a romance that quite literally never got off the ground. It was typical of my brother not to see that the whole thing was going to be a disaster right from the start. All right, so she's got a pretty face, but stick insects are not his thing at all and we had a good laugh about it and her afterwards. I didn't feel it at the time, but I'm ashamed of our behaviour now that I come to think about it. Amy must have been aware of our nudge, nudge, wink, wink whenever we met her afterwards. No wonder she avoided us after that disastrous date.'

'When did all that take place?'

'It must have been all of two years ago, and Bob and I were both younger and sillier than we are now.'

'Did you never bump into her when you went swimming with Monique?'

'No, she kept well away from us and anyway, soon after we started to do that, she took to her room, at least whenever I was about.'

'How about David? Where does he fit in?' Sinclair asked.

'He's a creep. He spied on us once when we were sunbathing. I saw the leaves of one of the bushes moving even though there wasn't even the suspicion of a breeze. I pretended to go back to the house while Monique put on a little show for him, circled round, got behind him, collared him and slung him in the pool.'

'What about afterwards?'

'I had a quiet word with Dr Cochrane, partly to cover my back if David complained, but also because, although a lot of people would say that that sort of thing doesn't mean anything in adolescent boys, I'm not so sure. One thing can lead to another and I don't believe that he just happened to see us on that one occasion, either, as he claimed. He also had a way of looking at Monique I didn't like at all.'

'How did Dr Cochrane react to what you said?'

'He just thanked me and said he'd deal with it. That wasn't the only time, either; Monique told me that David gave her the creeps and was always trying to look down her front.'

'Did he ever try to spy on you again?'

'Not that I was aware of. I kept a pretty sharp eye on him and we only went swimming when I knew he was out of the way.'

'Did you tell Monique that you had spoken to Dr Cochrane?' Sarah asked.

'No, I thought it would only embarrass her and she's a very trusting sort of person. She told me once that she felt sorry for David and that he seemed lonely. Anyway, he made a point of making himself scarce whenever I went round there afterwards.'

'It must be pretty quiet at the weekend round here, but we are interested to know whether you have ever heard a car coming along this road late on weekend nights.' Sinclair said.

'I'm afraid I never hear a thing at night; I sleep like a log. Anyway, once the park's closed and the planes stop flying overhead it's very quiet here.'

Soon after nine o'clock the following morning, Monique Durand took Amy's breakfast tray up to her room. Unlike most mornings, when the young woman was usually half asleep, she was obviously agitated. Her cheeks were flushed and her bedclothes were in an untidy tangle.

'Monique,' she said, her voice hardly audible, 'I'm feeling awful this morning, really terrible. I've just rung the hospital and Dr Clarke is sending an ambulance for me. Would you pack some things for me and please don't tell my mother until I've gone. She'll only get hysterical and I wouldn't be able to cope with that as well.'

Monique had never seen her like that before and was genuinely concerned, but she knew just what Mrs Cochrane was like and she followed Amy's instructions to the letter. It went without any problems at all. The ambulance crew, who arrived about an hour later, were cheerful and sympathetic, carrying

Amy down in the chair that they brought from the vehicle and even Mrs Cochrane, after one shriek of horror at the news, soon settled down when Monique reassured her that Amy was in good hands and that it was better for her to be safe in hospital rather than in the house with the police still wandering around.

Monique had just taken Mrs Cochrane a cup of coffee in the drawing-room after lunch and was back in the kitchen when the telephone rang.

''*Allo*.'

'Monique, it's Amy here. I need my mobile phone and I stupidly left it in my room as the result of all the hurry when the ambulance came. Do you think you'd be able to bring it to me as soon as possible? There is some money in the top drawer of the chest in my room and you can use that to take a taxi here and back and keep ten pounds for yourself. Please don't tell my mother – she'll only make a fuss.'

'*D'accord*. I wait for your mother to go to her club. She takes some coffee now. Are you feeling any better?'

'Just a little, thank you. You will get here as soon as possible, won't you?'

'Don't worry. I will.'

'Thanks, you're a star.'

Monique was smiling to herself as she went up the stairs to Amy's room after Mrs Cochrane had left for her club. The young woman's voice on the phone had sounded quite different, stronger and more decisive than usual and it would also be fun to go all the way up to central London in a taxi. The last thing she had expected, though, was to find the door of the bedroom locked. Monique hadn't been there when the ambulance men had been in the bedroom and Amy must have done it herself as she was leaving. She had never understood why, but Amy never liked anyone to go into her room when she wasn't there and had always locked the door when she used to go out for her weekend drives with the young man and on this occasion she must have done so as a matter of habit. She stood there for a moment, deep in thought. She knew that Mrs Cochrane would make a terrible fuss if she rang her at her club to tell her what had happened and to ask if there was a spare key. After all, she had promised Amy that she wouldn't. It was then that she remembered the serious-looking man, whom she had seen arrive earlier and who was in Dr Cochrane's study. She went downstairs and knocked softy on its door.

Jack Pocock was sifting through the contents of one of the drawers in Cochrane's desk when he heard it and he went across and opened the door. The scene-of-crime man may have always looked dour and unsmiling, but he was just as susceptible to the sight of a pretty young woman as the next man, let alone one wearing nothing but a thin white shirt above her denim skirt.

'Excuse me, sir,' she said and he was just about able to concentrate on what the French girl was saying in her heavily accented English about Amy having been taken to the hospital, that she had left her mobile phone in the bedroom and needed it urgently. She had also asked the girl to take it to her there by taxi, which she was happy to do, but the snag was that the bedroom door was locked.

With the girl in attendance, Pocock saw at once that it would be a simple matter to open it and the opportunity to take a look at the girl's bedroom was too good to miss.

'I think I will be able to unlock it for you,' he said very slowly, 'but I will need some instruments from my car and it might take me about half an hour. Will that be all right? Where will you be waiting?'

The girl gave him a dazzling smile. 'In the kitchen, *monsieur*, and thank you.'

Once he had got the go ahead from Sinclair on his mobile phone, he took the bunch of keys that he had found in Cochrane's desk, which he assumed correctly were spares for all the doors in the house, and was inside the bedroom within seconds of climbing the stairs. He found the telephone in a drawer in the bedside table almost as quickly, and twenty-five minutes later went back down to the kitchen.

'All done,' he said very slowly and carefully, 'I think it best for you to say that you found the phone yourself and, if anyone asks, just tell them that the door was unlocked.'

'*D'accord, monsieur*.'

To Pocock's profound embarrassment, the girl gave him a hug and the man knew there and then that he would never admit to anyone, most of all his wife, what effect the proximity of the young woman so close to him had had on him.

The following morning, after the two detectives had brought Tyrrell up to date with their inquiries at the hospital and Cochrane's house, Sinclair made a gesture in Pocock's direction.

'There was an interesting new development this morning and I think it would be best if I handed you over to Jack.'

Tyrrell nodded and the SOCO looked down at his notes.

'Soon after ten-thirty yesterday morning, sir, an ambulance arrived and took Amy Moffatt to Henshaw Hospital. Later on, early that afternoon, she rang the au pair girl asking her to bring her mobile phone to the hospital as she had forgotten to take it with her. She was quite willing to do so, but found the door to Amy's bedroom locked and asked me if I might be able to open it for her. I asked her what was the matter with the girl and she told me that when she took Amy her breakfast, the young woman said that she was feeling really ill and had rung Dr Clarke on her mobile. He told her that he was not in a position to come out to Roehampton to see her at home and that he would speak to Dr Clements about it with the recommendation that she should come into hospital for a few days to have a thorough check-up. He rang again half an hour later to say that Dr Clements had agreed and that an ambulance would come to fetch her shortly.'

'What was Amy's reaction to that?'

'The French girl said that she seemed quite relieved.'

'And Mrs Cochrane?'

'I didn't see her myself, but the au pair said that although she made a fuss about it, she thought the woman was more than happy not to have the responsibility for Amy, at least for some time until things had settled down a bit. Anyway, after Amy had departed, apparently she was sufficiently relaxed about the whole business to have gone off to her club.'

'And presumably you were able to open the door?'

'Yes, sir. I had already found a bunch of all the internal house keys in Cochrane's desk, but I thought that this would be a good opportunity to have a quick look at Amy's bedroom and pretended that I would need some kit from the car to do this job. That allowed me to say that I would need a good half hour to do it for her?'

'And?'

'After ringing Inspector Sinclair to get the go-ahead, I got into the bedroom very quickly and was able to have a good look at the girl's mobile. There was a facility for putting in a password, but it hadn't been activated and I was able to access the preset numbers on it and I also copied the photographs on it with the kit I had in Cochrane's study and I gave them to Inspector Prescott, who had been the one to interview Amy.'

Tyrrell nodded. 'Sarah?'

'We'll have to check all those phone numbers, but I can confirm that the girl in this picture is Amy.'

She passed the print across the desk and Tyrrell looked at the young woman who was leaning against a bar. Her hair was dishevelled, the top two buttons of her blouse had come undone, showing the tops of her breasts and she was sticking her tongue out at the person taking the photograph.

'There are a couple of others of her and there is also this one, sir.'

Tyrrell looked at the picture of a rather supercilious-looking young man, wearing a dinner jacket and with long, dark hair flopping over his forehead.

'Right,' he said, 'Sinclair, perhaps you'd give me a brief summary of where we stand now?'

The detective nodded. 'Obviously, Cochrane never believed that Amy had ME and also very much doubted that it was even an entity. Anyway, he was at a conference a week before he died and his daughter, Rebecca, told us that he had heard a paper about there being a good chance that a specific blood test for the condition might be developed in the fairly near future. If that proved to be the case, it followed that it might be possible to prove that it was a genuine medical condition and not just a label put on a particular type of neurotic adolescent girl or young woman. Such a test, though, was for the future, but once David, his wife's adopted son, told him that he had seen Amy sneaking out of the house on the Saturday night he was away, he had the idea of doing his own blood test on the girl. He probably suspected that she had been for a night out on the tiles on the Saturday night when he was away and if there was alcohol or even drugs in the sample, the diagnosis of ME would be thrown out of the window. Add to this, his view that making a diagnosis of a condition for which no specific test was currently available was potentially very harmful to psychologically vulnerable teenagers. It would also be dynamite in his hands with regard to his dispute with Dr Clements.

'His own daughter, Rebecca, is a senior registrar in medicine at St Gregory's Hospital and he gave her the sample, which he had taken on the Sunday afternoon, for it to be analyzed there. It showed clear evidence that the girl Amy had taken both cocaine and alcohol within the previous thirty-six hours.

'We also know from the au pair girl, who was always present when Dr Clarke, Dr Clements' senior registrar, came to do one of his regular domiciliary visits, that the man saw the plaster on Amy's arm and the needle mark underneath it and asked her why it was there. Did he put two and two together and, with his senior colleague, decide that Cochrane was of sufficient danger to their professional standing to warrant silencing him for ever?

'If the au pair, who was in the habit of listening at Mrs Cochrane's bedroom door when Dr Clarke was giving her updates on Amy's condition, is to be believed, there was a good deal more than that going on between the two of them and that they were having an affair.'

'I see,' said Tyrrell. 'Was the whole of that blood sample used up at St Gregory's?'

'I don't know, but Cochrane took a second specimen at the same time and put it in the fridge in his summerhouse, which Jack found and showed to us. Although it wasn't labelled with Amy's name, DNA tests would presumably confirm whether or not the blood was hers.'

'Any results on that yet, Jack?'

'Dr Tredgold is still working on it, sir.'

'How about Cochrane's study, Jack?' Tyrrell asked.

The man reached into his briefcase. 'I have here a copy of his will, sir, which I found in his safe. Luckily, it is an old model and the key was on the ring with the others which we found hanging from the padlock in the summerhouse. The will is dated only three months ago and, in summary, he's left the house and contents to his wife, with the exception of his two pianos, the grand in the sitting-room and the electronic one in his study, which he has left to Henshaw Hospital, together with any of his medical books and papers that his daughter, Rebecca, doesn't want. She also gets a substantial legacy, and some money has been set aside for David, specifically for his education. Amy gets nothing, although the au pair girl, Monique, has been left five hundred pounds in recognition of all her efforts in helping the family, particularly Amy.'

'Hmm,' said Tyrrell, 'I wonder what Mrs Cochrane's reaction to that will be and whether she will contest it.'

'I asked one of our legal team about that and they thought that the house and contents being worth more than Cochrane's other assets and the fact that she would also get half his National Health Service pension, it is very unlikely that she would succeed. She may also have received a substantial sum in the divorce settlement from her former husband.'

'Anything else?'

'We found some potentially interesting correspondence in one of the folders in the locked filing cabinet in the study. There was a letter from the headmaster of a private school, confirming a telephone call he had made in connection with Amy Moffatt's expulsion for drinking alcohol, taking ecstasy and smoking cannabis on the premises, for which they had a zero tolerance. His decision to expel both her and the boy she was with at the time would have to be confirmed by the board of governors, but he expected that they would support him. It also appeared that they had been having a sexual relationship. The two of them would be allowed to take their A-level exams on the school's premises with segregated supervision by a member of the staff.

'A copy of Cochrane's reply was also there. He stated that his wife, who was Amy's mother, had asked him to deal with the matter and enclosed a photostat of her letter confirming that that was her wish and that she understood that expulsion was inevitable. They both supported the school's action and very much regretted that Amy should have behaved in that way and that Cochrane would endeavour to get her into a rehabilitation programme. There was also correspondence in the same file with his solicitor, who had clearly helped with the drafting of the letter.'

Tyrrell nodded. 'Interesting, and inevitably one wonders if Amy is still seeing the young man and if he is the one in that photograph.'

'That seems quite likely, sir, and it's also possible that his number might also be one of those on the phone's memory, and they are all being checked.'

'And the girl is still in the hospital?'

'Yes, sir,' Sinclair said. 'She's in a single room and we thought it necessary to put a WPC in place as well. We neither want her running away nor having contact with that boyfriend of hers. To put it mildly, Dr Clements obviously doesn't like the idea, but I cleared it with the administrators and the chairman of the medical staff committee.'

'Anything more from your point of view, Jack?'

'Yes, sir, I found this book,' he said, taking the slim volume out of the large buff envelope. 'I doubt if I would have taken any notice of it had it been on one of the shelves, but it was in the safe and I thought that sufficiently unusual to bring it along with me here. There were also some entries on Dr Cochrane's credit card records there and I also thought they might prove to be of interest.'

Tyrrell glanced at it the book and the inscription on the flyleaf and handed it across to Sinclair together with the sheaf of papers. 'I haven't the time to look at it now, but you're our tame literary expert, Mark, and perhaps you'd let me know what, if anything, you think about it.' He glanced back in Pocock's direction. 'That's all then is it?'

'Not quite, sir. When the au pair had gone and I was alone in the house, I decided to have a proper look through both Amy Moffatt's bedroom and that of Mrs Cochrane. In both rooms I found some devices that I think makes it essential that we move Mrs Cochrane, the boy and the au pair out of the house as soon as possible to allow a thorough search to be made.'

'Intriguing,' Tyrrell said. 'What were those devices?'

'There were adaptors fitted to an electric socket in each room and I recognized them as plug transmitters. They allow voices to be picked up and all the listener needs to do is dial a number on a telephone, fixed or mobile, and listen in from any location. They're not all that expensive, at least for a man in Cochrane's position, a few hundred pounds, and fitting is extremely simple – one merely plugs it into an existing socket.'

'Hmm,' said Tyrrell, 'well done, Jack. Sarah, you're the one to have spoken to the girl at length and know her room, any views about who might have left the listening device there?'

'Well, the obvious person is Cochrane. Clearly he didn't believe that Amy was genuinely ill and might have wanted to keep tabs on her, particularly with reference to Dr Clarke's visits, or to listen in to her phone conversations. Did Monique drop any hints that the man was having an affair with his wife and did he monitor her room as well? What about Rebecca Cochrane? Did she put it in after her father's death or before. After all, she helped her father over the blood test and didn't believe in Amy's ME, either.

'Then there is David Cochrane. He is a computer geek, we know that he enjoyed spying on the two girls at the swimming pool and was it really just a coincidence that he saw Amy leaving the house when Cochrane was away at that conference, or had he heard her make the arrangement with her boyfriend on the telephone? Several hundred pounds seems a lot of money for a sixteen-year-old schoolboy to have to spare for the bug, but we know that he has an expensive model train system up in the loft. That doesn't come cheaply, either, and perhaps Cochrane was in the habit of giving him money for it.

'As to the others involved with Amy, her mother would hardly have bugged her own room, neither would she or Monique have had either the reason or the knowledge to set it up, and why should Dr Clarke have wanted to do it, either?'

'Did you find anything in Cochrane's study or bedroom to suggest that he had recorded what he may have heard, Jack?' Tyrrell asked.

'No, sir, but I haven't been to the man's office at the hospital yet and he may have kept the recordings there. I was planning to look into that first thing tomorrow.'

'Anything to add, either of you?'

'No, sir,' Sinclair said. 'I think that Sarah gave an excellent summary of the possibilities and, in the light of what Jack found, I agree with him that we ought to give the whole house a thorough going over. Although I also agree with Sarah's view that Cochrane is the most likely person to have put the bugs in those two rooms, I think that young David's computer, his bedroom and the rest of the house ought to be inspected thoroughly as well.'

Tyrrell nodded. 'I agree. Clearly, though, this needs to be handled both quickly and carefully and I'll deal with the interviews with the media; they are bound to prick up their ears more acutely once they hear that the family are being moved out. Arrangements will also have to be made for accommodation for Mrs Cochrane and the au pair now that Rebecca Cochrane has taken care of the boy and I'll deal with that.'

'May I make a suggestion about the au pair?' Sarah said.

'Of course.'

'The house belonging to the parents of Monique's friend is very near by. We have been there and know that they have a spare room and that would seem to be the ideal place for her as we also got the strong impression that she would be more than welcome.'

'That sounds very satisfactory. Just having to find one hotel room for Mrs Cochrane will be easier and less expensive. I'll liaise with you about it. What other plans do you both have?'

'We are proposing to interview the headmaster of Amy's school and David's form master and we'll also have to check the whereabouts of the two psychiatrists at the time of the murder,' Sarah said. 'As for Amy, I think it best if she stays where she is for the time being and we'll put pressure on the hospital authorities to make as sure as we can be that she doesn't do a runner. That will mean keeping a WPC outside her room. I'm pretty sure that we'd have Dr Metcalfe's support, although it might be a different matter as far as the administrators are concerned. What's your view, sir?'

'I'll have to think about that one,' Tyrrell replied. 'You make a good case, though. Any views, Mark?'

'I agree with Sarah that there's a real danger of Amy running away, with or without the help of that boyfriend of hers and if, as I suspect, Dr Clements is anxious to get her out of the hospital as well, I feel quite strongly that a police guard on her room should be kept in place.'

'Good point. Perhaps the best plan would be for me to get on to the member of the board who approached us in the first place. He'll certainly carry enough clout to overcome any objections from the administrators or the medical staff. Now, before you do anything else, I'd like you to go to see Tredgold. I had him on the line earlier today and evidently he's finished his work on the autopsy and he's got something in his lab that he'd like to show you.'

CHAPTER FIVE

Eric Tredgold, the forensic pathologist, looked up as his long-suffering secretary showed the two detectives into his office, raising his eyebrows slightly, but showing no inclination to get up out of his chair.

'Long time no see,' he said. 'I hope you are both flourishing and appreciative of my use of the vernacular, even though I have to admit it is a little dated. Sinclair, you're the lexicographical expert, perhaps you can enlighten me as to its origin.'

The detective wasn't in the least put out. 'You're right about it being dated, sir,' he said with just a hint of stress on the 'sir', 'it's said to have originated in the early nineteenth century as the result of the development of Chinglish, or pidgin English as some like to call it. The tea trade was flourishing with China at the time, as you no doubt know.'

Tredgold let out a loud guffaw. 'Not lost your touch, have you? How do you do it?'

'I used to trade one-upmanship over crosswords with Rawlings, one of your colleagues, when I was working for Thames Valley.'

'I might have guessed. I know that fellow of old. Good man, wasted in that small department of his, if you ask me. Miss Prescott, you look bewildered and I can't say that I'm surprised. Let us to business get. No doubt Pocock has already shown you these photographs, but let me refresh your memory.' The man took a print out of the folder. 'The victim appears to have been kneeling beside the pond feeding the goldfish, when he was hit on the occipital region of his skull and fell forwards into the water. This close-up shows the injuries to the back of his head and next the fracture of the occipital bone, but it was not the blow itself, that killed him; he drowned. There was water in his lungs.

'Pocock's team also found a faintly damp depression in the earth close to the path leading to the pond and there is now no doubt that a stone had been lifted from it. It was found over the fence of the neighbouring garden and it definitely was the murder weapon. There was blood on it and the DNA matched that of the dead man. Unfortunately, there was no other DNA on it or anything to identify the assailant, suggesting perhaps that he or she might have been wearing gloves, possibly leather or rubber ones as no fibres were found on the rock.'

'Would a woman have had the strength both to kill Dr Cochrane with that stone and throw it over the fence?' Sarah asked.

'We staged a little experiment in our laboratory garden, which proved the point, and I told Pocock not to mention it to you until I had tidied up all the details to my satisfaction. I have a video of the proceedings to show you, but before I do so, perhaps I should explain how I obtained a skull of similar size and thickness to that of the murdered man. You may or may not know that some public-spirited people, instead of being buried or cremated, donate their bodies to university departments of anatomy for the edification of students. Plastic replicas of all the bones are available, but are never quite the same as the real thing. Now, the skull that I was able to obtain was placed as near as possible in the same position as that of the murdered man when he was struck from behind.

'One of the scene-of-crime team, a young woman of slight build, as you will see in the video, was able to hit the back of the skull using the murder weapon, the stone that was found and identified by the victim's DNA on it, with sufficient force to fracture it. She was also strong enough to carry the missile to a rope fixed at the same height as the fence and throw it over to the other side.'

The pathologist slotted the CD into his laptop, twisted the machine to one side so that the two detectives were able to see the screen clearly and set it going.

'Convinced?' he said, when the clip had ended.

'I certainly am,' Sarah said. 'No footprints in the dew apart from Cochrane's?'

'Not of any use, I'm afraid. The path from the direction of the garage is paved and the grass near the body had been trodden on by so many people, Cochrane himself, the man who found the body and the ambulance crew, that nothing useful was found. In any case, by the time the SOCOs got there, the sun was up and most of the dew had gone except in shaded areas.'

'And there is no doubt that the stone was the murder weapon?'

'None at all.'

'Was Cochrane in good health apart from his injuries?'

'Yes, he was. Now, to finish, here are the X-rays of the skull of both Cochrane and the one that stood in for him, so to speak.'

He put the two films up on a viewing box on the wall and pointed out the two fractures.

'Not identical, but similar enough for our purpose, I think you will agree.'

'Have you been able to test the blood sample found in the summerhouse?' Sarah asked.

'Yes, and it confirms the finding of alcohol and cocaine and the DNA matches samples from the hairs on the brush that Pocock found in the girl's bedroom.'

'Who'd be a forensic pathologist?' Sarah said in the car on their way to Bristow College.

'The short answer to that is that it is ideally suited to someone with a personality of a man like Tredgold,' Sinclair replied. 'He only too obviously loves the whole package, which is fortunate from our point of view, as quirky and acerbic as he often is, he's top class at it.'

Guy Bracken, the headmaster of Bristow College, looked to be in his early fifties and was on the thin side, with a permanently anxious expression on his face. I wouldn't want to be a school teacher these days, let alone a headmaster, Sinclair thought. People were always taking about how important and rewarding a profession it was; he had no problem with the former, but rewarding! Constant worries about health and safety, discipline, media comment about the dumbing down of exams, frequent lack of parental support in the state system and financial pressures in the private one, all of those must be a nightmare.

'So you want to know about Amy Moffatt and the boy with whom she was involved?'

'Yes,' Sinclair said. 'As I mentioned when I telephoned, James Cochrane, the psychiatrist who married Amy's mother, but didn't adopt her daughter although she lived with him and his wife, has been murdered. We found some correspondence with you about Amy in Cochrane's study and as a result know that she was a troubled girl and that the start of it may have been her association with a boy called Rupert Mansfield. I have here a photograph of someone I believe to be him.'

The man nodded. 'Yes, that's Mansfield, all right. I think it would be best if I left the discussion about Amy to Marjorie Walker, who is head of the girls' side, who knew her well. Now, what about Rupert Mansfield? At times, I despair of the present day. You'd never think that a boy, despite having a good brain and nice looks, would have thrown everything away by breaking our cardinal rules by having sex with one of the fifteen-year-old girls, and encouraging her to take ecstasy, smoke cannabis and drink alcohol, would you? Such behaviour would also undoubtedly have blighted his own future completely, wouldn't it?

'Not a bit of it. He wasn't in the least contrite and his father, although apologizing for the boy's behaviour, obviously took the view that boys will be boys and that it would all come out in the wash. The most depressing part of it all, as far as Mansfield is concerned, is that it has. He is now working at one of the most prestigious finance companies in the City, his income must be in excess of a hundred thousand a year and he drives a fancy BMW.'

'It sounds as if he was a testosterone driven, spoiled brat, but was he more than that? Was there a vicious streak in him as well, do you think?' Sinclair asked.

'No, I wouldn't go as far as to say that,' Bracken said, 'and I put a lot of the blame for his behaviour on his parents, who obviously never set limits. It's perfectly true, though, that success and conformity at school don't necessarily mean success in the future, and Winston Churchill is a very well-known example of that; he confounded all of those who despaired of him when he was at Harrow.'

'Do you suppose that Mansfield will settle down eventually or indeed might have done so by now?'

'Very difficult to say and one could argue that there is a place for people like him in our society. After all, some very successful entrepreneurs have had troubled early lives. Different cultures, too, have different standards and family rules and that makes it difficult to apply fixed rules to everyone. I won't bore you with my views about that, but trying to maintain standards here that I personally hold to be important is no easy task. However, no one is forced to send their children to this school and the rules are made very clear before they start. Sooner or later, though, I wouldn't be surprised if we are taken to court with all the usual spurious fanfare about human rights. At least neither Mansfield senior nor Cochrane did that.'

'I have every sympathy with you,' Sinclair said. 'Did the whole business create a great commotion at the school?'

'No, and that was probably largely because the respective parents didn't want to make a fuss about it. We were also lucky that the discovery of those two's behaviour occurred near the end of exam time and it passed by without the national press being alerted. A few years back there might have been a grand announcement at a school assembly with pointed remarks about what happened to those foolish enough to break the rules, but that sort of thing has never been my style and I believe that the message got through effectively by more subtle methods.

'We know what effects the downgrading of cannabis have had and how taking it has become almost part of the culture, rendering it almost impossible to deal with the problem. Still, draconian steps over tobacco seem to be working and, knowing what would have befallen the two young people we are talking about had they lived in Singapore, maybe the total abolition of corporal punishment here was not such a good thing after all.'

'You may well be right,' Sinclair said, 'but achieving a situation like that in such a country can only be achieved when there is a smaller population and some form of dictatorship, or else one with strict control from religious leaders. I suppose other exceptions are very large countries in which local leaders in some parts are a law unto themselves.'

The headmaster smiled. 'Very true. Perhaps I ought to introduce the subject as a topic for our debating society.'

'Do you think that Rupert Mansfield might be capable of physical violence?'

'I have to say that I think that very unlikely. You see, I have a particular interest in rugby football here as I used to be a player and still do some coaching. Rupert was big for his age, strongly built and athletic, but when it came to the crunch he lacked bottle.'

Sinclair nodded. 'In our experience, physical violence is much more common in males than females and there are a number of reasons for it. Firstly, there is testosterone, making males more aggressive, secondly there is size and muscular development, and there is alcohol, although women are catching up with that. Male psychopaths are the ones who enjoy hurting people and often seem insensitive to pain themselves, others are on a very short fuse, are unable to control themselves and are often sorry for what they have done afterwards, and finally there are those who are driven to it because circumstances, such as the protection of loved ones, demand it. Women are not immune to violent impulses, but brute force is pretty uncommon, although drink and drugs seem to be changing that now.'

'Yes, I understand that, but I don't see Rupert Mansfield carrying out a violent act in cold blood, or even, for that matter, if provoked.'

*

Erica Hornby, the woman who had been Amy Moffatt's housemistress, looked to be in her early fifties and Sarah took to her at once as she came across as being straightforward and cheerful. Remembering her own exclusively spinster school mistresses, Sarah thought that the woman, who had two daughters of her own, long since grown up, in bringing them up, must have gained a greater insight into the behaviour of adolescent girls and how to deal with them than they had.

'Yes,' the woman said, 'I remember Amy only too well and I worried about her a lot. The openly rebellious and naughty girls are child's play to deal with compared to those, like Amy, who on the surface seem passive and conforming, but underneath are up to all sorts of nefarious activities. She wasn't by any means the least intelligent of her group, but she was one of the lowest achievers. Trying to motivate her was like chasing a feather – there was nothing to get hold of. If one tackled her head to head, she used to look at one with a doleful, passive expression and provoked in me an almost irresistible desire to shake her.

'Quite honestly, I was staggered when the sex thing was discovered. She was just as passive in her general behaviour as she was in class and perhaps that was her secret attraction to someone like Mansfield. He was clearly supercharged in testosterone terms and finding someone who would do literally anything in the sexual repertoire that he demanded of her must have been just what he was looking for. That's pure speculation, of course, and I suppose it's possible that he introduced her to drugs to help him to get his way with her.'

'That's very interesting,' Sarah said, 'because although I have only talked to Amy briefly, I got very much the same impression. Finally, may I ask you if you can see the girl having been responsible for an act involving physical violence?'

There was a long pause. 'My immediate reaction to your question was that the very idea is absurd, the main reason being that, when she was here, Amy was very thin and had very poor muscular development. I even wondered at one time if she was suffering from anorexia. However, she was an arch manipulator and I could just about see her persuading someone to act on her behalf.'

'Rupert Mansfield, for example?'

The woman smiled. 'You'll have to ask one of the masters about that.'

Paul Richards, David Moffatt's form master at the large private day school, which was only three miles or so from the house in Roehampton, met the detectives in one of the small rooms that the senior staff used for interviews.

'David Moffatt has been a cause of some concern here,' he said. 'The boy is extremely bright in some ways, but he also has personality problems, hardly surprising in view of his background. Dr Cochrane came to see me and the headmaster when he applied for a place for David a couple of years ago and was very frank about the situation. One might have expected a lot of jargon from a psychiatrist, but he was both direct and clear in his assessment of the boy. He pointed out that nothing was known about his parentage – he was abandoned as a baby, having been left in the porch of a church when he was only a few days old – and from then on it was a succession of foster homes. He was finally adopted by Cochrane's wife and her first husband when he was eleven. Cochrane told me that they had wanted a boy of that age to balance their only child, a girl a few years older. Mrs Moffatt, as she was then, was unable to have any more children herself. Cochrane himself thought that in all probability they chose David because he was attractive physically with his blond hair and blue eyes. Evidently, though, when Mrs Cochrane first saw him, she didn't realize that he was quite seriously short-sighted and with adolescence and the need for thick glasses, he rapidly lost his early good looks.

'Various reports about him stated that he was both quiet and studious, but that was an understatement. He had great difficulty in relating to other children, particularly girls and that included Amy, their natural daughter. In confidence, Cochrane told me that one of the reasons for David's adoption was that when Amy was going through a difficult time in early adolescence, her parents felt that having a brother younger than her would give her a companion and make her less petulant and rude. Cochrane was pretty tactful about it, but he clearly thought with hindsight that it was doomed to failure. The two children were like chalk and cheese. Amy, the girl, was sulky and self-centred, whereas David was studious, antisocial and only happy when playing with his computer and the train set that Cochrane helped him to set up. Eventually, they were getting on so badly together that the girl was sent to a boarding school and David came here.'

'Did he settle in quickly?'

'It is quite easy to be anonymous in a large day school like this. There aren't the cliques that develop in boarding schools, games are not so important and are not forced on those with no liking and less aptitude for them. The boys come from quite a large area in the vicinity and what sexual problems there are centred at home rather than here.'

'I was going to ask about that. Did Cochrane mention any problems in that direction with regard to David?'

'The question did arise, because I am well aware of what can happen in care homes, but Cochrane told me that there was no reason to believe that he had been abused in that way. He did say that David seemed to have no interest in girls, but was quite relaxed about it, saying that he didn't need to tell a school master that boys developed at very different ages in that regard.'

'When did you last see Cochrane? I was wondering if there had been any recent problems with David?'

'It's curious that you should ask that because only recently, it was about two weeks ago, when the man attended a parents' evening on his own, he hinted that he had had some trouble with David in a sexual context. It was nothing serious, he said, he had dealt with it himself and the incident was over. He obviously didn't wish to talk about it in any detail and, in any case, I found his being a psychiatrist distinctly inhibiting with regard to that particular topic and didn't press him in any way about it.

'We did meet last term, it must have been about four months ago, and then it was merely to discuss the boy's academic progress, which was highly satisfactory in science subjects, but less so in the humanities. As I recall, there were no issues about his behaviour here or at home at that time. David, with his lack of social skills, thick glasses and lack of interest in games, might well have been bullied, but there were no problems of that nature here as far as I could tell. If David wore contact lenses, he would be quite nice-looking, but I didn't feel it was my place to make any comment about that. Had he been in the slightest bit interested in sport, I might have raised it, but he wasn't and isn't and I felt that that was up to the boy himself and Cochrane to deal with it.'

'How does he appear to have reacted Cochrane's death?'

'I did worry about that and only the other day told David that if he wanted to talk about it, either I or the chaplain would be only too happy to see him at any time.'

'How did he respond to that?'

'Just told me that he was all right and he seemed quite happy with the arrangement of his staying with Dr Cochrane's daughter for a few days. I met her very briefly the first day she brought him here and she gave the impression of being a highly competent person and to have everything under control.'

'Yes, I felt the same about her and I'm sure he's much better with her than in a hotel with his mother. He shouldn't have to stay with her for very long as it is our aim to get the family back to the house as soon as possible.'

'I think we're going to need a bit more ammunition before we tackle that smooth fellow, Clarke,' Sinclair said as Sarah was driving them back from the school, 'but why don't we pay a call on the acerbic Dr Clements this evening?'

It was a little after 9 p.m. when the two detectives arrived at the block of flats in Beckenham and Sarah pressed the button on the entryphone panel.

'Yes,' said a disembodied voice.

'Inspectors Prescott and Sinclair, Metropolitan Police,' Sarah said. 'May we come up?'

'At this hour?'

'Yes, what we have to say to you is important.'

'It's on the fifth floor.'

There was a loud click and the door opened a fraction. Dr Clements was waiting for them as the door of the lift opened.

'This is outrageous,' she began, 'and—'

'We could have seen you at the hospital or at Scotland Yard,' Sarah said, 'but thought that you might not welcome possible local or press interest. If we were wrong, we'd be happy to fix up one of those locations tomorrow.'

For one moment, the woman seemed about to say something, then obviously changed her mind and stepped aside.

'You'd better come in.'

One of the doors off the lobby led into a small dining-room

and, pointing to the two chairs on the other side of the table, she sat down herself.

'Well, what is all this about?'

'While Dr Cochrane was away at a weekend conference a short time ago, at which I gather you were present as well, Amy Moffatt left his house in the small hours of the Sunday morning and went to a nightclub. She was seen both leaving the house and returning and, as a result, when Dr Cochrane was told about it directly he got back, he took a sample of Amy's blood on the following Sunday and had it analyzed at a laboratory away from his own and your hospital.

'Tests showed that Amy had taken significant amounts of both cocaine and alcohol. Dr Cochrane had kept a second specimen himself, which we found and the results have been confirmed in our laboratory. Clearly, that evidence puts the diagnosis of ME in serious jeopardy and, had he not been murdered, who knows what that might have led to.'

'Are you suggesting that I had something to do with Cochrane's death?'

'We are not suggesting anything at the moment,' Sarah said, 'merely looking into all the circumstances surrounding your ex-colleague's death. It would, however, be most helpful if you would tell us what you were doing between say 6 and 8 a.m. on the Sunday before last when Dr Cochrane was murdered.'

The woman hesitated for a moment. 'Being a Sunday morning after a hectic and busy week, I was having a lie-in. As I recall, I had breakfast in bed.'

'Is anyone able to confirm that?'

There was a long pause. 'I do share this flat with someone and....' There was a long pause. 'She is a very nervous person and I fear she might break down if I weren't present when you talk to her.'

'As an experienced psychiatrist, I am sure you'll understand that that won't be possible,' Sarah said. 'Should she not be prepared to see us on her own, we can always arrange for her to meet us with her solicitor present at the local police station. Might I suggest that you ask her to come back here with you and we'll put the alternatives to her?'

'This is outrageous.'

Sarah stared at the woman unblinkingly. 'If that is your view, we will have no alternative but to follow the course of action I mentioned.'

'Very well.'

Dr Clements got up, left the room and some minutes later there was a soft knock on the door. Sinclair went across the room, opened it and gave the woman, who was standing diffidently outside, a smile.

'Do come in and sit down over there. My name is Prescott, Inspector Prescott, and my colleague here is Inspector Sinclair. Your name is?'

The woman lowered her head and her reply was almost in a whisper. 'Phyllis Avery.'

'And you live here?'

'Yes.'

'Do you know why we're here?'

'Yes, Dr Clements just told me.'

'So you know that we're enquiring into the murder of one of her colleagues, Dr James Cochrane?' The woman nodded. 'We know within an hour or two when it occurred and all we need from you is confirmation that Dr Clements was here on the morning of the Sunday morning before last between the hours of 6 and 8 a.m.'

'Yes, she was.'

'Could she have left the flat between those hours without your knowledge?'

'Not possibly.'

The flush on the woman's face spread all the way down the neckline of her dress.

'There's something worrying you, isn't there? Would you like to talk to us again away from here?' The woman nodded and Sarah tore out a sheet from her notepad and wrote down her name and phone number on it. 'This is for my mobile and feel free to ring me at any time. Where do you work?'

'I'm Dr Clements's health service hospital secretary.'

'Is there anywhere else we might meet where you would feel more comfortable?'

There was a very long pause and the woman looked round to make sure that the door was firmly closed.

'I will be working at the Royal Society of Medicine next Monday morning looking up some references for Dr Clements and we could meet in the lobby there, say at eleven. I have to be back at the hospital by half past twelve to take dictation for letters from her clinic. Do you know where it is?'

'Yes, we do and we'll meet you there at that time.'

'You won't tell Dr Clements about it, will you?'

'No, we won't.'

The psychiatrist reappeared a minute or two after the woman had left the room and Sarah looked at her very directly.

'That clears the question of where you were on the morning that Dr Cochrane was murdered,' she said, 'but before we go, perhaps you'd let us have your thoughts about Amy Moffatt in the light of what we know about her now.'

'Amy is a manipulative and devious young woman and under the present circumstances I will of course consider the best course of action with regard to her future in consultation with Dr Clarke, who knows her better than anyone else at the hospital. As far as I'm concerned, I'm not having anything more to do with her management and she'll be leaving Henshaw Hospital as soon as I can organize it.'

'She will have to stay in the single room where she is at present for the time being, and that has been agreed with the authorities at the hospital,' Sarah replied. 'Her mother, brother and the au pair are being moved out of the house while our team search it and for the moment there doesn't seem anywhere else for her to go. We will, too, be interviewing her at length in the very near future.'

'That room is one of the facilities on my ward and I'm not having that deeply disturbed young woman there – it's needed for another patient who is genuinely ill.'

'Nevertheless, as I told you, she will have to remain there

for the time being and one of our WPCs will be in close attendance. It's only too clear that you disapprove of that course of action, but may I remind you that we were called in by the chairman of your board and I don't imagine that he would take kindly to any hint that you are not prepared to cooperate fully with our inquiries. In any case, a decision as to whether she will be staying there and for how long is not, I believe, in your hands, it having been accepted by the chairman of your medical staff committee and academic board.'

'This is outrageous. I'll—'

'I suggest you take the matter up with the hospital authorities and it might also be in your interests to consult your solicitor before you do so and even your medical defence society – I presume that you are a member of one. As to Dr Clarke, your senior registrar, he also has some potentially difficult questions to answer.'

'What's that supposed to mean?'

'I'm quite sure you will find out in due course.' Sarah pushed back her chair and got to her feet. 'Now, we won't disturb your evening any further.'

Sinclair grinned at his colleague as they made their way towards their car.

'I reckon you enjoyed that.'

'I certainly did. That odious woman gets right up my nose.'

When they got back to the flat, Sinclair saw his briefcase on the table by the phone in the small hall and more from habit than for any other reason opened it and saw the large, buff envelope that Pocock had given him in which was the book that the man had found in Cochrane's safe.

'Good Lord!' he said, 'I'd forgotten all about this.'

He took the book into the sitting-room and, sitting side by side on the sofa, the two of them examined it. The slim volume was bound in leather, dyed blue, and in gold lettering on the front was printed *Poems of Love and Respect*. Inside, on the title page was written neatly in ink:

To J from A,
'That best portion of a good man's life,
His little, nameless unremembered acts of kindness and love'

'I don't know that quote, but perhaps it's in the index. It's the "A" that interests me. Is it a patient, a student, just an admirer, even, dare I say it, a lover?'

'I imagine that psychiatrists must get a lot of gifts like that,' Sarah said.

'Perhaps they do, but why was it in the safe?' Sinclair ran his finger down the index. 'Yes, here we are.' He found the page and nodded. 'It's Wordsworth, "Lines Composed a Few Miles Above Tintern Abbey". That's a strange coincidence; it's where I interviewed that SAS NCO in the Kate Farrant case.'

'How, though, is it linked with the note Jack has left with these credit card statements?'

'What does Jack's note say?'

Sarah picked it up and read from Pocock's neat script.

'"Regularly, once a month, with occasional breaks, for the last several years, there have been payments to a private hotel in Matlock for Saturday night stays in a single room for bed and breakfast, which occurred roughly once a month. However, a little under a year ago on a number of occasions the pattern changed from the booking of one single room to two."'

'That's interesting,' Sinclair said, 'and from what she told us, the other room was not for Rebecca. Cochrane's visits to his mother would not only have been a golden opportunity for Amy to take advantage of them for her trysts with her boyfriend, but does it also suggest that Cochrane had a girlfriend, and was it she who gave him the book? There's nothing urgent to be done over the weekend, so why don't we check out that hotel? I've wanted to visit Chatsworth House for a long time and I'm pretty sure that it's not far from Matlock.'

'What a good idea! That book is certainly worth chasing up, we both could do with a break and our next firm appointment isn't until our meeting with Phyllis Avery on Monday morning. I'd better give Tyrrell a ring to tell him what we propose to do; there's never any harm in making something like that official – one never know who's snooping on whom these days.'

CHAPTER SIX

THE LIMES HOTEL on the outskirts of Matlock was quite small, family run and was set in an acre of ground surrounded by trees and with a fine lawn surrounded by beds of shrubs and roses, all kept in immaculate order. What had obviously been the front garden had been converted into a car park and several vehicles were there when they arrived.

'How terrible!' the comfortably built, middle-aged woman at the reception desk said, when Sarah had told her about Dr Cochrane's murder. 'It must have been in the paper and on TV, but we've been run off our feet this summer and Alan and I missed it. The doctor was such a nice quiet gentleman and after all these years, all of ten, I would say, he's become quite a friend and the dogs always make a fuss of him. His mother, you know, has been in a home quite close to here for all that time. He told me long ago that she no longer recognized him, but he never abandoned her like some I could mention and said that the sound of his familiar voice seemed to give her some comfort. The owner of the home, whom I know a bit, also told me that acknowledgement of the efforts of the staff, which he always made a point of showing with a large box of chocolates every Christmas, was greatly appreciated. It can't be an easy task looking after people like that.'

'No, I'm sure it isn't,' Sarah said. 'What did Dr Cochrane do for the rest of his time here?'

'He loved walking and told me that being able to stretch his legs on the hills round here and having a break from the hospital recharged his batteries, as he put it. I was so pleased when about six moths ago he started to bring his niece with him. She is a rather diffident, quiet sort of person, quite unlike the doctor's daughter, whom I didn't take to at all, even though I only met her a couple of times when Dr Cochrane was away and that was a long time ago. I found her brusque to the point of rudeness. The niece could hardly be more different; she's very quiet and is such a tidy person and as Mrs Talbot, one of my cleaners, said after one of her visits, "you'd hardly know that she'd been in her room."'

Sinclair raised his eyebrows slightly, but to Sarah's relief, the woman obviously didn't appear to have noticed.

'I even wondered if she was convalescing from a serious illness – she always looked so pale and tired. Anyway, I'm sure that Dr Cochrane valued her support; he seemed so much more relaxed than when he used to come here on his own.'

'Do you think Dr Cochrane's niece will come here now that he's dead?' Sarah asked.

'I certainly hope so and she'd be very welcome.'

'Is the nursing home far from here?'

'No, only ten minutes' walk. That's why Dr Cochrane used this hotel.'

'Perhaps you'd point out the way for us. I realize that we won't be able to communicate with Mrs Cochrane, but we can hardly come all this way and not see her. If nothing else, from what you've said, I'm sure that Dr Cochrane's niece would appreciate it.'

'I'm quite sure that she would. She seemed such a caring person and the two of them had such a nice relationship.'

The two detectives were most impressed by the nursing home. The great majority of the patients were suffering from dementia and it must, they realized, be very difficult for the staff to keep cheerful and enthusiastic when they got such a small amount of feedback from the people they were looking after.

'What's your impression of the close relatives of the people here?' Sarah asked the senior nurse on duty.

'Some, like Dr Cochrane, are very supportive of our efforts. He took the trouble to thank us every time he came and always gave the staff a handsome present every Christmas. Others expect standards they never even begin to supply themselves when their relatives are at home and the worst are those who constantly criticize both the food and the care provided. I'm not saying that we're perfect and I don't need to tell you about some of the recent scandals concerning homes like this, which unfortunately have had the effect of making relatives even more critical and on the look-out for faults. The staff here are not saints, but we all do our very best and should there be a slip-up we correct it. It's not an easy job, this, and a little appreciation of our efforts goes a long way. It's often those relatives who only blow in every few months who are the worst nit-pickers. The owner here won't put up with it and his answer is that if they are that unhappy about the way things are run, clearly it would be better for all concerned if they found somewhere else. One woman made a real fuss and reported the home to the local health department. The result was an inspection which we passed with flying colours and that had a salutary effect, at least for some time.

'On the other hand, though, we do have a lot of help from volunteers. Someone comes to play the piano regularly for sing-songs, there is a retired man who used to be a member of the Magic Circle and, being in his late seventies and the widower of a woman who had dementia, he knows at what level to pitch his act and there are sufficient people who are well enough to appreciate his efforts. One has to balance the need to stimulate and entertain patients against pushing those, like Mrs Cochrane, who are best left in peace with little more being done for them other than to take them down to sit in the shade in the garden. Even then she needs someone to be with her the whole time in case she should wander off.'

'I understand that Dr Cochrane came to Matlock with his niece a few times. Did she visit the old lady with him?'

'No. Mrs Parker, who runs the hotel where Dr Cochrane used to stay and who helps us with fund raising by holding coffee mornings and bring and buy sales, told me about her. It seems that she is not well and that being the case, I think he was wise to tell her not to come with him. It's not as though Mrs Cochrane would have benefited from it. Would you like to see Mrs Cochrane yourselves?'

'Having come all this way, I think we should and we can always give a report to Dr Cochrane's daughter.'

It was every bit as unrewarding as the two detectives had expected. The frail old lady was in an armchair in one of the sitting rooms, staring vacantly at the wall opposite her, not even turning her head when one of the nurses attempted to introduce them as visitors.

'The people I feel sorry for,' Sinclair said as they walked back to the car, 'are those relatives who feel they can't keep away, even though they must know that all they are achieving is to pull themselves apart. My own mother, who, as you know, is still in rude health, will have none of it; she has made a living will, she does not want to be resuscitated if she has a disabling stroke or develops severe dementia and luckily my brother and I are fully in tune with her over that.'

'What about Cochrane's devoted niece?'

'No prizes for guessing who she really is, her having left her initial so conveniently on the flyleaf of that book. We clearly need to have another chat with her in the near future.'

'Why don't we go round to her flat tomorrow evening after we've seen Jack Pocock and Andrew Clarke?' Sarah said.

'Good idea. We also need to see Amy before too long and I wonder if you'd take that on. She's likely to say more if you see her on her own and perhaps we ought to interview Rupert

Mansfield before you do so, and there's also our appointment with Phyllis Avery. Now, let's put all that on one side; there are more immediate and rewarding plans to be made.'

Away from the tyranny of mobile phones, which were firmly switched off, and pagers, which had been left behind in London, the remainder of the weekend was just what both of them needed. They had a walk round the town, a slap-up meal at an excellent restaurant and afterwards ... afterwards, in the bedroom of the excellent hotel they had found a few miles up the road from the town, they were able to forget all about murders and illness, real or imagined, and were able to let themselves go without fearing a ring on the telephone. The repeat performance the following morning was even better and was followed by a proper English breakfast, a visit to Chatsworth House and a long walk in the magnificent grounds.

Phyllis Avery was waiting for them in the lobby of the Royal Society of Medicine when they arrived a minute or two before eleven the following morning.

'Is there a coffee shop near here, where we might sit and have a chat?' Sarah asked.

'Yes,' the woman replied. 'There's one in Oxford Street and it's only a short walk from here.'

As the woman sat down at the table and as Sarah looked round to catch the attention of the waitress, who was serving a table a few feet away, out of the corner of her eye she saw Phyllis Avery reach across her chest with her right hand and very gently rub the livid bruise, which had become visible under the short sleeve of her summer dress.

'Did Dr Clements do that to you last night?' she asked. The woman pressed her lips together and nodded. 'Why not tell us all about it?'

Phyllis Avery had been in her middle thirties, worn down by having looked after her querulous, invalid, widowed mother for the previous twenty years, when her life changed completely as a result of the demanding old woman's sudden death. She had just enough money to take a course in keyboard and computer skills and, to her surprise, not only did she find that she had an aptitude for them and mastered them quickly, but, even more, she enjoyed the challenge of the medical secretarial course that followed. She knew about Henshaw Hospital – it was quite close to the council flat where her mother had lived – and more in hope than expectation, she applied for a post there.

Fed up with the rapid turnover of the young women they had been employing, the head of the medical secretaries department at the hospital was both impressed by the excellent report given by the principal of the secretarial college on the serious-looking older woman and by the fact that she had taken the trouble to find out exactly what the hospital did in advance of the interview. To Phyllis's surprise and delight, she got the job and for the first year or two she worked for the junior doctors, mainly in the out-patient department, then earned some more money by helping the postgraduate students with the preparation of their theses and scientific papers. It was thanks to that, when Dr Clements's secretary left, that she was asked if she would like to take that job on. Apart from dealing with the psychiatrist's correspondence, another important part of the work and one which she particularly enjoyed, was to help with the preparation of Dr Clements's articles and lectures, by looking up references in the library of the Royal Society of Medicine for her.

The rest of it started during a conference in Brighton. She had gone up to Dr Clements's room late on the first evening to go over the slides for the woman's presentation the next day and to discuss some of the papers that had been read earlier, during which she had made notes. It had been a long and exhausting session and when she was offered a drink from the minibar, she gladly accepted. It went on from there. Totally unused to alcohol, she was feeling giggly, other worldly and deliciously relaxed and it was then that it happened. She wasn't completely ignorant – how could she be after all that she had read about in the research work she had done for Audrey Clements? – but the reality of what happened that evening was quite another matter. The other woman was immensely experienced and knowledgeable and was in no hurry, gradually weaving her web. Other occasions followed and finally Phyllis moved into the woman's flat.

Audrey Clements was in many ways a bully, but there were many compensations. The woman quite often went to conferences overseas and Phyllis stayed with her in first-class hotels, visited foreign countries and widened her experience of life, but all the time was never left in any doubt about who was in charge, all her activities not only being arranged, but also commanded by the psychiatrist.

Phyllis knew all about Dr Cochrane and his views on ME; how could she avoid it when Audrey was always speaking about him and in such a disparaging way? It was such a pity, she thought, because he seemed to be such a nice man, much respected by the medical staff, students, porters and secretaries alike. In her time at Henshaw Hospital, Phyllis had become very knowledgeable about many aspects of psychiatry, not least the ethics involved. What, she wondered, was Audrey doing taking on Amy Moffatt as a patient, particularly after the ill-judged article that she had written about Cochrane's views on ME and the real threat of libel action against her? The answer wasn't difficult to find; Audrey was not only both blinkered and rigid in her views about ME but many other things besides, not least her firm belief in the innate superiority of women.

That wasn't all of it, either. After having worked for most of one afternoon in Dr Clements's office on the ward, checking some references and preparing some tables for a paper that the psychiatrist was writing, Phyllis Avery had developed an unpleasant migraine and, having taken a Panadol with a glass of water, she was sitting back in her chair with the window open and the blinds down, when she heard voices from outside in the corridor.

One of the young nurses was talking to Dr Prior, the senior house officer who was working on the ward. She didn't hear every single word, but it was very clear that Dr Clements had carried out an intimate examination on Amy Moffatt without a chaperone being present and that the girl had been very distressed. That was bad enough, but her feeling of betrayal was even worse. Audrey had told her so many times that she was the only one for her and how could she assault a young and vulnerable patient and what was she going to do about it? Finally, to her shame, she did nothing, reasoning that Dr Prior would know how to handle it.

She had tried to put it out of her mind, but with the news of Dr Cochrane's murder and the visit from the police, it all came flooding back. When Audrey had come into the sitting-room to tell her that the detectives wanted to see her, the woman gripped her arm with such force that she nearly cried out.

'Tell them that you were in bed with me from 6 to 9 a.m. the morning Cochrane was killed,' the woman said. 'That's what they'll want confirmed and it won't be difficult for you because it's true. You won't say a word about anything else connected with us, our relationship, the hospital and, in particular Amy Moffatt. Is that absolutely clear?'

Audrey gave her arm another very hard squeeze and although that was bad, what was even worse was the woman's aggressive attitude after the police officers had left.

'Why were you so long in that room with those detectives? You didn't tell them anything, did you?'

'Of course I didn't. I wasn't there for any longer than you and all they asked me was where I worked in the hospital and what I did there.'

'And what did you say?'

'Just that I was a medical secretary.'

'But not that you worked for me?'

'Yes, but what else could I do? They probably knew already and if they didn't, they would find out as soon as they asked around at the hospital.'

'All right, but you didn't say anything about Cochrane or that slut of a girl.'

'Of course not.'

'And our relationship?'

'Only what you told me to say.'

'Well, don't even think of going into any more detail than that. This whole business is nothing to do with you and the less you say to them the better should they decide to question you again. Now, get yourself ready; after all that's happened recently I'm feeling stressed and I'm ready for something special.'

'No, please, not that. You know how I hate it.'

'Shut up and do as you're told, otherwise I might lose my temper and you'd like that even less, wouldn't you?'

'None of what I've told you will get back to Audrey Clements, will it?'

'We'll be interviewing Amy ourselves very soon and once she knows that Dr Clements wants nothing more to do with her management, she may well tell us what happened when she was examined by her. From your point of view, I see no reason to suppose that you will need to be involved with this whole business again unless a formal signed statement is needed confirming that you were with Dr Clements at the time when Dr Cochrane was murdered.'

'But what am I going to do myself?'

'That is entirely up to you,' Sarah said. 'The hospital must have a personnel officer who should be able to help you if you decide to leave Henshaw Hospital. Medical secretaries with your experience must be greatly in demand if you decide that you'd be better off away from psychiatry. As for your personal life, there may be a sympathetic counsellor or social worker at the hospital to assist you in deciding what to do and if you'd prefer to see someone elsewhere, I'm sure you have enough experience now to get in touch with one yourself.'

Pocock was his usual taciturn self when they arrived at Cochrane's office at the hospital, giving them a grunt and a nod in response to their 'good mornings'.

'Perhaps I'd better deal with the photographs first,' he said.

'Photographs?'

'I found a flash card in that small safe over there and I'll bring up some of the pictures on it for you on my laptop.'

There were image after image of Monique, the au pair girl and her friend, Jess Foster. They had all been taken both in and around the pool in Cochrane's garden and were in sharp focus, showing every detail of the girls' anatomy and what they had been getting up to together.

'Presumably the boy, David, took them, but have you any direct evidence to confirm that?' Sarah asked.

'Well. The flash card would certainly fit his camera, but that would be true of any number of others. However, the boy had already downloaded some of the images on to his computer so I don't think there can be any reasonable doubt about it. There were also some pictures of his model train set on the card.'

'Have you found any other cameras?' Sinclair asked.

'Amy Cochrane had one hidden under some jumpers in her chest of drawers and there are, what one might term, adult pictures on that card as well. I also found an old Leica in Cochrane's study. I went through his various photograph albums and it was clear that they had all been taken with the same instrument, including the most recent, all of which were obsessively labelled with the weather conditions, the focal length of the lens and the timing. We haven't carried out a thorough search of the boy's bedroom yet, but we made quite sure that he wasn't able to take his camera, computer or any CDs with him when he went off with Dr Cochrane's daughter. The keen female sergeant who was there when he left also made him turn out his pockets and searched his suitcase before he left.'

'How did he react to that?'

'He made quite a fuss about it, but he was told that unless he shut up, he would be subjected to a strip search.'

'Do you think she would have gone that far?'

'No, I don't, but the boy didn't know that and I think he was terrified by the thought.'

'I see,' she said, raising her eyebrows slightly. 'We know that

Jess Foster complained to Cochrane about David and I wouldn't be surprised if the man put two and two together, suspected that the boy had taken photographs of the girls and then found the flash card in his room. When do you suppose the pictures were taken?'

'It must have been within the last few weeks,' Sinclair said. 'I've had a look at that pool; the water isn't heated and, with the cool spring and early summer, I can't see those two girls frolicking about like that before then. What did Cochrane do when he discovered those pictures, I wonder? Whatever sanctions he took must surely have been expended for David to have been prepared to tell him about Amy's midnight flit.'

'Maybe he used that bit of information as a bargaining weapon with his father,' Sarah said.

'That's a good point. Anything else, Jack?'

'I have an idea about those sanctions and I'll show you and the Chief Superintendent when we go to the house. I've already mentioned the pictures on Amy's camera; care to take a look at them?'

Sinclair did so then passed them across to Sarah, giving her a quizzical look. 'One can't deny that the young man, presumably Rupert Mansfield, is well endowed. No wonder Amy looked shattered after her Sunday afternoon trysts. What have you done with the camera, Jack?'

'It's already back where I found it, sir, and no doubt you and the Chief Superintendent will decide what to do with it.'

'I thought I'd put all this sort of thing behind me after I stopped working on the vice squad in London, but I was wrong. What other rabbits are you going to pull out of your hat, Jack?' Sarah said, carefully avoiding looking at Mark Sinclair.

'Well, ma'am, there are some recordings in the safe here, which prove that it was Cochrane who put the listening devices in both Amy's and his wife's bedroom.'

'Perhaps we ought to listen to them both. Have you had the opportunity to edit them yet, Jack?'

'Yes, I have, ma'am, but I'd better let you have the originals as well for you to show to Mr Tyrrell.'

Sinclair nodded. 'Good point, but perhaps it would be better if you took them yourself as we will be interviewing other people later today and the security of those recordings is of the utmost importance.'

'Very well, sir, I'll deliver them myself on my way back to the house.'

'How much longer is it likely to be before you've finished in there?'

'Not more than two or three days, I'd say.'

Sinclair nodded and Pocock gave them both earpieces. The recording from Amy's room was mainly concerned with telephone calls to her boyfriend, Rupert Mansfield, making arrangements and timings for their evenings out. Apart from them, her conversations with Dr Clarke and Monique were innocuous, although her little girl voice, when she was with the psychiatrist, Monique and during the occasional visits from her mother, was in striking contrast to her confident tones when having jocular and intimate conversations with Mansfield.

As for Jean Cochrane, Monique had not been exaggerating about the woman's trysts with Andrew Clarke and, even more valuable for their purpose, she liked to use his name when she was pleading with him not to punish her, which he did noisily and to her obvious enjoyment and satisfaction.

'Good work, Jack.'

'I'll be going back to the house immediately I've finished here, sir, and I'll let you know what we discover as soon as we've tidied up all the ends.'

'Right. Tyrrell may want to be there as well and, in any case, we'll need to consult him about timing with regard to the occupants' return.'

Pocock nodded. 'Finished with these recordings, have you?'

'Yes, thank you, for the time being at any rate.'

The two detectives decided to wait until Dr Clarke had finished his morning clinic and saw him a few minutes after he had finished dictating his letters.

'There have been some developments since we last saw you and we thought it was time to have another word with you,' Sarah said.

Sinclair looked at the man closely as they sat down opposite him. Although a casual observer might have said that he looked relaxed and confident, the detective was quite certain that the man must have heard something already that morning. The twisted smile and slightly cynical expression was still on his face, but in some subtle way he seemed to have lost a good deal of his self-assurance.

'Feeling in need of a consultation, are you?'

Sarah stared at him until the man suddenly dropped his eyes and shifted his position uncomfortably in his chair.

'I don't know whether Dr Clements has already had a word with you this morning,' Sarah said, 'but I should warn you that you are in serious trouble.'

'Presumably you're talking about Amy Moffatt,' he said, looking straight at her. 'The management of her case has been the entire responsibility of Dr Clements and I have followed her instructions to the letter. I have never even considered examining the young woman without the presence of a chaperone as the au pair girl, Monique, will no doubt be happy to confirm. The fact that Amy has deceived us is one of the occupational hazards of practising psychiatry, a discipline in which tests, such as scanners, have no part to play other than to exclude physical illness.'

Sarah waited until the silence became oppressive and then said: 'I'm not talking about Amy, Dr Clarke, I'm referring to her mother, Mrs Cochrane.'

'What do you mean?'

'Dr Cochrane must have suspected that after your visits to Amy you were sharing, how shall I put it, some recreational activities with his wife. How did we find out about that? Not only did he have his suspicions, but they were strong enough for him to have put a listening device in her bedroom, from which he made certain recordings, which are now in our possession.'

All the colour had gone out of the man's cheeks and he

began to fidget in his chair. 'I had absolutely nothing to do with Cochrane's death.'

'I hear what you have to say, but it would do your cause no harm if you were to tell us what you were doing on the Sunday morning of his death between 6 and 9 a.m.'

There was a long pause. 'I was alone in my flat.'

'Are you able to prove that?'

'No, as I've just said, I was alone.'

'Did you have any phone calls that night?'

'I had just one, a call from the SHO on our firm about a patient who was in a hysterical state and that was at about 9.30. I was able to suggest appropriate action without having to go in to the hospital myself.'

'Nothing later on.'

'No.'

'Do you live there alone, or do you have a flatmate or partner?'

'My wife was unable to put up with the demands of my job and she divorced me eighteen months ago. I now live alone.'

'Do you have a regular girlfriend?'

'No, I don't – the job again.'

'Have you and Dr Clements discussed the situation following Dr Cochrane's murder and the revelations about Amy?'

'Only to the extent of her telling me that I'm not to have anything further to do with the young woman for the time being and she also told me that it would be wise to put my medical defence society in the picture.'

'And you have done that?'

'Yes.'

'What was their advice?'

The man looked at Sarah very directly. 'That I should take certain courses of action, one of which I have not followed so far, but I now think that the time has come for me to do so. I would like to meet you again in the presence of my solicitor to give you some information about Mrs Cochrane and her household.'

CHAPTER SEVEN

DR CLARKE ACTED far more quickly than they expected and the senior registrar and his solicitor arrived at the Yard in the early afternoon of the following day.

'Would you have any objection to this interview being recorded?' Sarah said.

'No,' the man said, 'provided that Miss Franks, here, and I can vet the transcription.'

'We would have no problem with that.'

'Right.'

After Sarah had set the scene, listing the place, the date and the exact time, Andrew Clarke began.

'I undertook domiciliary visits to the Cochrane household following the instructions of Dr Clements, the senior consultant on the firm for which I work at Henshaw Hospital. The purpose was to monitor the progress of Amy Moffatt, the natural daughter of Mrs Cochrane, who was suffering from ME and was not well enough to undertake follow-up visits to the hospital. The whole situation was delicate as Dr Cochrane, also a consultant at the hospital, did not accept that ME was a physical illness, the exact opposite of the stance taken by Dr Clements.

'I got on well with Amy during my domiciliary visits, but thought it best never to see or examine her alone in view of the delicacy of the situation. However, after each consultation I made a point of telling Mrs Cochrane about Amy's progress. I found her both sympathetic and extremely physically attractive and as a result of that, a sexual relationship started between us. I will not attempt to excuse our behaviour, but for different reasons we were both unhappy and frustrated in our personal lives and what we did together fulfilled a need.

'I had met David, who had been adopted by Mrs Cochrane and her former husband, on a few occasions when I was at the house and we got on well, although our meetings were always very brief. During one of them he showed me his model railway set-up in the loft. It was extremely elaborate and I was very impressed. A few weeks ago, just as I was leaving, he ran down the stairs and spoke to me. He didn't mince words. He told me that he had had a row with his father, who had refused to help him with anything else he wanted to buy for the foreseeable future. He went on to say that he knew what I was getting up to with Mrs Cochrane and he urgently needed two hundred pounds in order to extend the circuit in the loft and that that was not an excessive request in view of what had been going on. The medical authorities and no doubt James, as he called him, would not exactly approve if they knew what had transpired between the two of us.'

'How did you react to that?'

'I told him I needed to think about it and, after agonizing about it for the rest of that day, I decided to see Dr Cochrane and confess to what had been happening, which is what I did the following day.

'I was dreading the man's response, but to my surprise, he was remarkably calm and reasonable. The bones of what he said was that I should continue my regular visits to Amy, but that I was neither to see nor even speak to Jean or David again and that he would deal with any problems between the two of them and himself. He told me that as far as he was concerned the matter was now closed and that while I had not committed any crime, my behaviour had been unacceptable, not least because I was a doctor and had abused my position. He finished by saying that I would be well advised not to be such a bloody fool in future.'

'And have you followed his advice?'

'To the letter. However, then came the terrible news of Cochrane's murder, and after the interview with you I decided to consult my medical defence organization.'

'And has either Jean Cochrane or David tried to contact you again?'

'No.'

'Why do you suppose that was?'

'I can only assume that Cochrane tackled both of them himself.'

'And how about Mrs Cochrane? What do you suppose her reaction will be when she discovers that her frolics with you were recorded on a listening device?'

'It depends entirely on what Cochrane said to her and did about it. For me, it was nothing more than a bit of a fun and relaxation with an uninhibited older woman and I believe that the same was true as far as she was concerned. She was seriously sexually frustrated and she admitted to me that marrying Cochrane had been a bad mistake. True, he gave her and the two children, Amy and David, security, and the house, garden and location were just what she had always wanted. The down side was that although in many ways he was a nice man, he was serious-minded and no fun at all, particularly in bed. It was clear to me that the man had a low libido and he looked upon sex as a duty rather than a pleasure, but to be fair, he was under a great deal of strain at the time. There were pressures at the hospital, not least with regard to his row with Dr Clements, he had the worry of Amy, and David was also difficult. He was also probably clinically depressed, which would explain a lot.

'Of course, I understand that what I was doing with Jean was unethical, even though she was not a patient of mine, and I see now that it was also stupid in the extreme. I am not making excuses, but I am also stressed and unhappy, which leads me to be flippant with the people like you, as you've no doubt already noted. The same is true with regard to my attitude to the senior people at the hospital, which no doubt explains why I am stuck at my present ceiling. I have applied for consultant posts, but I am convinced that Dr Clements has compromised my chances by writing lukewarm references and no doubt having a quiet word with the heads of departments to whom I have applied.'

'Why would she do that?'

'Because she has come to depend on me as I take the lion's share of the clinical work off her shoulders, while she swans off to conferences and buries herself in her particular obsession, which is, of course, ME. I have had interviews, but my general experience in psychiatry has suffered from having worked too long with adolescents and that has counted against me. As I've told you already, eighteen months ago I went through a divorce – my wife decided that living with a stressed psychiatrist with poor future prospects was not for her. She met someone else and that was that.

'As for Jean Cochrane, it started with my flirting gently with her, she responded and was not only prepared to go along with any variation you choose to mention, but actively encouraged me. She told me that at first Cochrane had fulfilled his marital duties, if you'll excuse the pompous euphemism, but then the whole thing began at first to become predictable and boring and then fizzled out altogether. She found what we did together exciting, fun and a relief after all the stress she was going through with both Amy and David. It didn't mean anything more than that to either of us. Amy is, after all, her natural daughter and Cochrane was very unsympathetic about her ME, not even considering it to be a genuine condition, and that Amy was using her symptoms as an escape from the responsibilities inherent in growing up and earning her own living. The fact that he proved to be correct in her case doesn't alter the fact that he was, in my view, to a considerable degree responsible for Amy's behaviour by failing completely to understand adolescents and their vagaries.'

'So what is your assessment of Amy and the outlook for her future now that Dr Clements has no doubt told you that she has been taking drugs with her boyfriend?' Sarah asked.

'I have to admit that she deceived me completely. There being no specific test for ME, one is dependent on the literature on the condition and, most importantly, on one's experience of other cases.'

'And she fulfilled the clinical criteria for that diagnosis?'

'Yes. She looked tired and drained, was underweight, weak, and her behaviour fitted with Dr Clements's wide experience of the illness.'

'And you are convinced yourself that ME is a specific entity?'

'Oh, yes. I have no doubts about that at all.'

'And in view of the information about her that has been uncovered, what diagnosis would you put on her now?'

'If you require me to put a label of any sort on her I can only say that she is manipulative and devious. She gave me a litany of sob stuff about how unhappy she had been at school and how unsympathetic and what a bully Cochrane was. She also clearly hated David, the boy whom her natural parents adopted. After Jean's marriage to Cochrane, she considered that she was being controlled by him and indeed the only person in the house she had any time for was the French au pair girl and even that was coloured by envy.'

'Envy?'

'Yes. She was envious of her youth, her looks, her figure and cheerfulness. I don't think she had any idea that the girl was gay, which was immediately obvious to me.'

'And what about Amy's future?' Sarah asked.

'One has to hope that she grows up and that what is happening now is the catalyst for improvement. I wouldn't be too optimistic, though. It is unfortunately very often the case that once a psychopath, always a psychopath.'

'And what about David?' asked Sinclair.

'I feel sorry for him, even though he tried to blackmail me. It was very clear to me that nobody at home liked him, he doesn't appear to have any friends and he is at a day school that has very high academic standards. All that sort of thing can be very difficult to take for an awkward, intelligent adolescent. I have to admit that I only ever spoke to him in passing, until the time he showed me his model railway up in the loft, which has been the cause of a lot of all this grief. I have to say I was very impressed with the set-up, which was extremely elaborate.'

'It must have also cost a good deal of money.'

'I asked him about that when I was up in the loft with him and he told me that nowadays with such a variety of computer games available, model railways were thought to be old hat and were not as popular as they used to be. As a result, there were plenty of bargains to be found on eBay. He said that Cochrane had also helped and he had saved up his pocket money for some of the more expensive items. I wasn't to know then that he had ambitions to extend the set-up even further, or that he would go to such lengths to do so.'

'How much was Dr Cochrane involved in setting it up in the first place?'

'Initially, he was the driving force behind it. Evidently, he was keen on the idea of boys of David's age having a hobby and he encouraged him by cleaning out the attic for him and going up there at regular intervals, seeing how the lay-out was developing and, as I said, giving him generous financial help from time to time.'

'Did you ever meet Cochrane's natural daughter, Rebecca?'

'No, I didn't, but Mrs Cochrane told me about her, saying that she is a superior, managing person, who is direct to the point of rudeness and had no time at all for Amy and didn't hesitate to pull David up in front of the rest of the family if he was rude to her father or even just uncommunicative. For God's sake, what adolescent doesn't have moods from time to time, but I never even considered that David might go to the length of trying blackmail?

'As for Cochrane, according to his wife, he tried to bribe David to work harder and behave better by not only giving him the money for his purchase of additions to his railway set-up, which I mentioned just now, and he also used to play chess with him. Although he is computer literate himself, he pretended not to be "to boost David's morale", as he put it, by asking for his help with his own system. Needless to say, he also supplied funds for the boy to keep his software up to date.'

'Did it succeed in getting the boy to like him?'

'No, it didn't. According to Jean, David thought Cochrane was patronizing him and trying to buy his affection.'

'If we are able to satisfy ourselves that you had absolutely nothing to do with Cochrane's death, where will you stand with regard to your future at this hospital?'

'I haven't been Dr Clements's senior registrar for nearly three years without having got to know her well. Let me just say that when blame for the fiasco over Amy Moffatt is apportioned, even if it becomes clear that in no way were either of us responsible for Cochrane's death, I know where it is likely to fall and it won't be on her shoulders.'

'I don't suppose I need to tell you this, but I should warn you not to try to contact Amy either here or at home,' Sarah said. 'She will be leaving the hospital as soon as we are able to arrange it.'

'What did you make of him?' Sarah asked, when the man and his solicitor had departed.

'When he mentioned his solicitor and the medical defence organization, I thought he was going to clam up on us completely and I most certainly wasn't expecting him to be so frank, making no attempt to deny what he had been doing with Jean Cochrane, nor that he had been deceived by Amy. He also seems to have no illusions about his boss and I think he's right. I can see Clements doing a comprehensive job on making as certain as she is able that as much of the blame for the fiasco lands on anyone other than herself.'

'I agree with that,' Sarah said, 'but I wonder about Clarke's account of Cochrane's reaction to the revelations about his wife. Would he really have been so cool about it? I doubt it somehow and we only have Clarke's word for it.'

'Yes, that's a good point,' Sinclair said. 'Maybe I got taken in by his open manner.'

'Anyway, one thing we can't put off any longer than tomorrow at the latest is seeing Amy at the hospital.'

'I agree,' Sinclair said. 'The hospital authorities must obviously be wanting to get rid of her as soon as possible, but before she leaves Tyrrell will want to look over the house with us and Jack Pocock. And what about Mansfield?'

'Amy was able to tell him that she was back in the hospital when she first arranged for her admission to it, but he hasn't made any attempt to see her and the WPC has made sure that he's not able to get in touch with her in any other way. Amy and her room have been searched thoroughly, her mobile has been confiscated and no visiting of any sort allowed. I suppose we could always put her in protective custody, but I'm sure Tyrrell would prefer us not to have to do that, as it would ratchet up the press interest.'

'Right. Why don't we see Alison Prior this evening and then tackle Mansfield tomorrow morning. That might give you more ammunition when speaking to Amy in the afternoon? I'm quite sure that you would be able to get more out of her if you are alone with her and then perhaps you might also have a word with Dr Metcalfe to let him know what's going on. I am quite happy to explain the situation to Tyrrell and it's not as if he will need both of us to be present when Jack shows him round the house. If he is able to make a decision about when the occupants will be allowed to return, I'll give you a ring at the hospital, preferably before you see Metcalfe.'

'That makes sense.'

Alison Prior opened the door of her flat on the chain when Sarah rang the bell that evening.

'May we come in? Sorry to descend on you like this, but we'd like to have a chat with you about Dr Cochrane away from the hospital.'

The young woman let them in, showed them into the sitting-room and then, when they were sitting on the sofa, perched herself on the edge of an upright chair as she faced them, her tension obvious from the twitching of her left eyelid.

'On looking through Dr Cochrane's study at his house,' Sarah said, 'we found a slim volume of love poems with a touching dedication on the flyleaf. We also discovered details of his credit card transactions which showed that there were a number of occasions over the last few months when he paid for two rooms at the hotel near his mother's nursing home in Derbyshire, rather than just the one, which had been the pattern over the previous several years. You were there with him, weren't you?'

'Yes,' she said, after a very long pause. 'but there wasn't anything sordid about it.'

'Tell us about it.'

*

Alison Prior was an anxious and nervous only child and remained so throughout her adolescence and when she went to medical school. Her father had died when she was only five and after that, she lived alone with her mother. It was not that they were short of money, but the woman had gone into a state of chronic depression and Alison led an almost solitary existence. While not being bullied at school, she never made close friends there and it didn't help that there was never a question of anyone being invited back to the house. The pattern continued at medical school. She was extremely bright and hard-working and a charismatic female psychiatrist at the hospital began to take an interest in her and her future career. The woman became a role model for Alison and fired her enthusiasm for the discipline. She obtained a higher degree in general medicine, and after she had decided to specialize in psychiatry was delighted to obtain a post as senior house officer at Henshaw Hospital.

She was so disillusioned by her first six months on Dr Clements's service that she very nearly decided to give up the speciality altogether, but after a further six months on a different firm she was promoted to registrar and started to work for Dr Cochrane. After that, everything changed. He was always keen to hear her views on the patients on his ward and in his clinics, discussing their symptoms in detail with her and at the end of that six months, she knew that adult psychiatry was what she wanted to do.

It wasn't only that; one evening he took her out to dinner at his London club. The unaccustomed wine, even though she only had two glasses, loosened her tongue and on a sudden impulse it was then that she told him that one of the nurses on the ward had confided in her about the way Dr Clements had behaved towards Amy in carrying out an intimate examination without a chaperone when she was first admitted to the hospital.

Alison hadn't been on the ward herself at the time, but the young nurse on duty had found Amy in tears after Dr Clements had left and it was then that the girl told her what had happened. Almost immediately, though, she obviously had second thoughts about what she had said and asked the nurse to promise not to tell anyone about it. The nurse felt she had to do something and that was why she spoke to Alison, who had no reason to disbelieve her. She had no idea how to handle the situation, but after talking to Amy herself the following day, she decided to do nothing. She didn't tax Amy directly about it, merely threw out hints to the effect that if there was anything in particular worrying her, all she had to do was talk it over with her and she promised that it would be just between the two of us and not recorded in the notes. Amy failed to respond and so she left it at that.

'Why then did I break my word that evening and speak to Dr Cochrane about it when I went out to dinner with him?' Alison said. 'I think it was because I was a little tipsy and I felt that Amy might be in further danger. By then, too, I had got to know Dr Cochrane really well and I was sure that he would know the best way to handle the situation.'

'How did he react?'

'He listened carefully to what I said, told me that I had done the right thing in telling him about it and that he would deal with the situation himself.'

'How did he do that?'

'I don't know and didn't like to ask. In any case, Amy had appeared to settle down quite well on the ward within a day or two of it having happened and soon afterwards she was back at home. Perhaps he thought that no great harm had come from the incident and may well have decided to let sleeping dogs lie. Amy also obviously liked and trusted the senior registrar, Dr Clarke, who had taken over most of her care. Of course, to my shame, I had only told Dr Cochrane about it a long time after it had happened and he may well have concluded that it was just hearsay and that stirring it up many months after the event would be highly unlikely to achieve much and might run the risk of alienating him even further from Amy.

'It was only a few weeks after that dinner that he told me that I was looking pale and tired and that it was time that I got away from London for a weekend and got some fresh air. He explained about his mother's Alzheimer's disease and that he normally stayed in a small hotel near the care home and that he was sure that he would be able to get a room for me too if I would like to come with him. I was pretty naive even then, but not so naive that I didn't realize what might happen, but what the hell! I couldn't remain a desiccated spinster for ever.

'I was even able to laugh at my fantasies when he behaved with perfect propriety towards me that weekend, introducing me to the owner of the hotel as being his niece. Those two days were a magic time for me. He bought me some proper boots and as a start took me for a not too demanding walk in the Peaks. We had long talks about music, finding that we had a mutual love of baroque composers and he told me about some of his adventures at university where he had belonged to a climbing club, scaling peaks in the Lake District and in Scotland and a memorable visit to the Alps.

'It was on our third visit that it happened. On the night that we arrived, when we went upstairs after dinner, he said: "There's something I'd like to show you in my room."'

Alison Prior looked across at Sarah, a flush on her cheeks. 'In theory, I knew a great deal about sex, how could I not, having studied and practised most aspects of psychiatry for the best part of two years and listened to patients' accounts of it in all its variations. The practical, though, so to speak had virtually passed me by completely. What happened could have been an anticlimax, or even a disaster, but it wasn't in any sense. He didn't hurry me, allowing me plenty of time to get used to showing my body to him and looking at and touching his and then it happened. Many patients have told me that the first time could be at best a disappointment or at worst a nightmare, but that wasn't true for me. For the first time in my life, I knew what it was like to let go completely and allow the sensations to flood over me.

'It was something I had needed to experience in order to develop as both an individual and as a doctor, he told me, and that I would now be a more secure and complete person. No doubt that might sound cynical to you, but he meant it and it was true. I grew up during that evening and the second time the following morning it was even better. It must sound childish, but even going back to my room to ruffle up the bedclothes and use the basin in there added to the excitement. When we went walking after he had seen his mother, he told me to forget about guilt, that was for him to cope with, although he knew that his wife had been unfaithful for a long time and didn't really feel any himself. He also told me not to worry about Amy, saying that he hadn't given up on her and never would.'

Alison Prior looked very directly at Sarah without dropping her eyes as she continued. 'I know what I've just told you must sound sordid, a married psychiatrist having sex with virginal junior colleague, but it wasn't like that at all. I'm not so naive and starry-eyed as to believe that it was true love; it was two stressed and deeply unhappy people having a brief interlude that was, in their quite different ways, the very opposite of either of those things. I will never forget that weekend, nor the two that followed it, nor will I ever regret them.'

'Have you any idea who might have wanted to kill Dr Cochrane?'

'Well, I tried to talk to Amy about him, but she didn't respond at all. I suppose one could argue that once she knew that he had discovered that she had faked her illness and what she had been up to with her boyfriend, she might have wanted to kill him, but I can't see her having done so, let alone in such a violent way. Did she persuade her boyfriend to do it?

Yes, Dr Cochrane knew what she was getting up to in the end and he told me about it. What about his wife? In addition to telling me that she had been unfaithful to him, he also said that their relationship in that way had foundered irretrievably and he understood why she had found sex elsewhere. How could I reasonably complain, he said to me, when the same thing has now happened to me?

'Dr Clements? I am biased, as I dislike that woman intensely, but I am convinced that she did assault Amy sexually and I feel deeply guilty about failing to do anything about it at the time. She ought to have been struck off. Surely, too, other vulnerable young girls are likely to have been her victims and maybe still are, however careful she has been to disguise what she is doing. It was a great relief for me to have told Dr Cochrane about it and I did so again on one of our weekends together. He again reassured me, saying that as Amy hadn't complained about it either to him or me and that I had only heard about it second hand, from an inexperienced nurse at that, he had decided that there was nothing he could do about it. That wasn't to say, he went on, that he was denying that it had probably happened, but he thought it would be more damaging to Amy to stir up things so long after the event than to let sleeping dogs lie.

'The thought has gone through my mind that if Dr Clements had assaulted Amy in that way, she might have decided, even with the long time interval and with the threat of a libel suit against her, that there was a possibility of Dr Cochrane finding out about it and maybe any other similar acts. Would that have been enough for her to decide that he needed to be eliminated? I can't see Dr Clements doing anything like that herself, let alone in such a violent way, but did she pay or persuade someone else to do it for her? I know that all this must sound vindictive and fanciful and it's true that, as I said, I dislike the woman intensely, but I haven't been able to get those thoughts out of my mind.

'I don't know enough about Dr Cochrane's family and friends to say anything further and I've probably said far too much as it is. Will my affair with him have to come out? Let's not beat about the bush; if it did, it would be the end of my career.'

'I can't give you any promises, but if we are satisfied that it had nothing at all to do with his murder, I don't see why it should.'

Sinclair waited until they were in the car on their way back to the Sarah's flat. 'What did you make of her?' he asked.

'She was obviously besotted by Cochrane, but I believe what she said. It fits in with a lot of what we've discovered so far.'

The finance house where Rupert Mansfield worked was in a new office block in the City and the two detectives went there the following morning. A young woman, wearing a navy-blue suit, was sitting at a desk in the lobby and smiled at them as they approached.

'How may I help you, sir, madam?'

'We'd like to have a word with Mr Rupert Mansfield,' Sinclair said.

'Have you got an appointment?'

'No, but I'm sure he'll be prepared to see us.'

'I'll put you through to his secretary.'

She consulted a list which she took out of the top drawer of the desk and pressed out a number on the telephone.

'Heather! A lady and a gentleman to see Mr Mansfield.... Right; I'll hold on while you ask him.' There was a long pause before the young woman looked up and put her hand over the mouthpiece. 'He's busy at the moment, sir.'

'Perhaps it would be best if I had a word with the secretary myself,' Sinclair said.

She handed the instrument over. 'My name is Sinclair; it won't mean anything to Mr Mansfield, but perhaps you'd tell him that I and my colleague would like a word with him about Amy Moffatt and that it's not appropriate to discuss the matter over the phone.... Yes, I'm sure he's busy, but it won't wait. Just mention the name of Amy Moffatt to him, would you, please?'

There was another long pause and then the secretary came back on the line.

'If you'd go up to the fifth floor in the lift, sir, I'll wait for you there.'

'Thank you.'

The secretary, a woman who appeared to be in her late fifties, was waiting for them on the landing outside the lift and looked at them unsmilingly.

'If you'd care to come this way, sir, madam?'

Rupert Mansfield glowered at them from behind his desk as they were shown into his office.

'Now, what the hell is this all about? It'd better be good.'

'Police,' said Sinclair, holding out his warrant card. 'I'm Inspector Sinclair and my colleague here is Inspector Prescott. I take it that you're Rupert Mansfield.'

'What if I am?'

'We need to know what you were doing between the hours of 6 and 8 a.m. on the Sunday two weeks ago.'

'Why do you want to know that?'

'Do I really have to spell it out? You were responsible for introducing Amy Moffatt to both sex and cannabis, as the result of which you were both expelled from your boarding school. Subsequently, you knew that she was faking illness and you continued to see her by pretending to be another friend from school and deliberately deceiving Dr Cochrane. It was quite a good act, wasn't it? Neither he nor anyone else at the house thought that the well-dressed, clean-cut young man with the impeccable manners and interest in religion, who took the ailing Amy out for drives on Sundays, was you. Hardly surprising when you claimed to have been at school with her and to have known how badly she had been led astray by a nasty piece of work by the name of Rupert Mansfield. It was your Christian duty to help her to come to terms with it all and with prayer and faith she would be sure to get better.

'They liked all that, the Cochranes, didn't they? It was such a contrast to the evil Rupert and a clever touch was Amy's reluctance to be taken out. It was no wonder that she looked shattered when she got back. We know from some of the photographs that she was unwise enough to keep that it was pretty energetic stuff that you got up to together. You and Amy, though, weren't satisfied with just that, were you? You also like clubbing and she wanted something with more pep than cannabis and added cocaine to her repertoire. It was careless of you both to take photographs of each other in that club and not to protect them on her camera with a password, not that that would have prevented us from bypassing it, although it would have taken some time. Perhaps, having got away with it for so long, you didn't even realize just how stupid you were being.

'Amy had the ill luck to be spotted coming back home in the small hours, though, which led to Cochrane carrying out a blood test on her, which showed evidence of both alcohol and cocaine intake. That firmly put paid both to the ME and her assumed innocence. She used her mobile phone to tell you what Cochrane had done, didn't she? Not surprisingly, that was that as far as you were concerned and you decided that the time had come to "black flag" her, to use a motor racing term with which I am sure you are familiar. Now, you may have thought originally that Cochrane was a pompous old fool, but it was now obvious that he had you by the short and curlies, a rather vulgar expression to be sure, but graphic and to the point nonetheless. As a result, did you get together and hatch the plot to batter him to death?'

The man gave a sniff. 'Don't be ridiculous. The business of Amy's supposed ME had gone too far and I wanted out. She wasn't a bad lay, but I had moved on and she hadn't. It's true that I didn't like Cochrane. I thought he was a pompous old windbag and you should have seen the way he reacted when I pretended to be the upright, God-fearing, earnest young man, whose duty it was to succour and support Amy. I was hardly able to keep a straight face. Despite that, I had no reason to want him dead.'

'That's as may be, but it would be in your interest to tell us where you were and what you were doing that Sunday morning between 5 and 8 a.m.'

There was a long pause. 'I was with a girl, if you must know.'

'Her name?'

'She called herself Tess, but I don't suppose that was her real name.'

'Perhaps you'd explain.'

'I met her at a club and we went back to my flat in Chelsea.'

'Which club was it?'

'It's called "Rock and Rave" and it's in Soho.'

'Been there often, have you?'

'No, it's a new one – a mate told me about it and that was my first time there. When I was standing near Tess, she told me that the place was a load of crap and I got the message. That's when I suggested that it would be more fun back at my flat with a drink and something suitable on one of my CDs and let me just say that she liked the idea.'

'Did money change hands then or later?'

The man made a gesture of disgust. 'Do you really believe that someone like me has to pay for it? I never have and never will. No, she was just up for it, that's all.'

'At what time did she leave your flat?'

'Later on that morning, after we'd showered and had breakfast. It must have been about half past nine.'

'Where did she go after leaving you?'

'I don't know. I offered to drive her to wherever she wanted, but she preferred to go on her own. I imagine she found a taxi in Sloane Street. There's a rank there and it's only ten minutes' walk away.'

'And where exactly is your flat?'

'I have the basement and first floor of a house just off Cadogan Square.'

'So it's unlikely that anyone would be able to corroborate what you've told us.'

The man gave them a look, a combination of a smile and a sneer. 'I value my privacy and it was one of the reasons for my taking on the tenancy of the place.'

'And you didn't get her phone number or make any plans to see her again?' Sinclair asked.

'No, I didn't.'

'Are you in the habit of having one-night stands?'

'Not as a rule, but if I meet the right girl....'

'What would your father have to say about something like that? I gather he was very disturbed and angry about your expulsion from school.'

'I understood that. He was naturally very upset about the publicity at that time, but what I do now in the privacy of my own place is not something that should or does concern him, providing that I am discreet about it. He goes along with that, and for my part I don't interfere with his private life at home or away from it, either.'

'But surely what you were doing with Amy for such a long time hardly comes into the same category, does it? And what are you proposing to do about her now?'

'I never want to see her again. She was all right to start with and then she became a needy, clinging vine and nothing but trouble.'

'That's a bit rich coming from you, isn't it? You started it way back when you were at school – yes, we've had a talk to the authorities at Bristow College – and it's quite clear that you led her on originally and now, when the going's got rough, you've decided to drop her like a stone. Is that right?'

The man flushed, seemed about to say something and then slowly got up from behind the desk. 'Have you quite finished, Inspector? I have to attend a meeting shortly and I need to do some work on my presentation. Now, if you'll excuse me?'

'You're not thinking of going anywhere in the next week or two, are you, Mr Mansfield? We may need to see you again and we need the address of that club, and don't tell me that you don't know it. We would also like your home address and landline phone number as well as that of your mobile.'

The man scribbled the information down on the notepad in front of him, then pressed the buzzer on his desk. 'My visitors are leaving, Miss Halstead,' he said when the woman came into the room. 'Would you show them out, please?'

'What a poisonous young man!' Sarah said when they were

back in the car. 'But does he really mean to dump Amy, just like that?'

'One could say that he has done so already, but is it just an act? Did he murder Cochrane and, if so, why? I very much doubt if Amy would have told him about the blood test, because it seems unlikely that she knew the significance of it. I can also understand why he wants to bail out now and I very much doubt that he would have wanted to do so earlier on when he was having his cake and eating it, so to speak?'

'I agree,' Sarah said, 'and I reckon that he's just the sort of man not to have been entirely satisfied with a girl like Amy. I wouldn't be surprised if "variety is the spice of life" in that context is very much his philosophy. Is he a murderer? Like you, I very much doubt it? And what about his alibi? I doubt if it's even worth trying to check it, unless someone at the club recognizes the photo Jack got off Amy's mobile. I'm quite impressed by the WPC who's one of the team keeping an eye on Amy in the hospital, so why don't we get her to pay the place a visit and have a word with the manager and one of the bouncers. They might just have noticed Mansfield.'

'Good idea.'

CHAPTER EIGHT

THERE WAS A different WPC in uniform outside Amy Moffatt's single room and inside, Amy, wearing hospital pyjamas and a dressing gown, was sitting in a chair by the side of her bed, watching television.

'You'll be going back to your mother's house in Roehampton very soon, Amy, quite possibly tomorrow,' Sarah said, having switched the set off and pulling up a chair directly opposite the young woman. 'After that, you'll have to stay there until we've finished our enquiries. Let me make the situation quite clear so that there is no misunderstanding. You were in the house when Dr Cochrane was murdered, by then he knew that you had cocaine and alcohol in your blood and also that the diagnosis of ME was something you or your boyfriend had cooked up. I don't know exactly what your motives were, but you were being waited on hand and foot, you had what one might term recreational drives into the country at weekends with your solicitous boyfriend and clandestine visits to night-clubs. It wasn't such a bad life, was it, and you no doubt had the satisfaction of deceiving the man whom you disliked intensely and who was pushing you into getting training for a job you no doubt thought was beneath you. Did you also enjoy the visits from Dr Clarke? Perhaps you're an exhibitionist as well and got a kick out of being examined by a good-looking doctor.

'You're no fool, are you, Amy, and once Dr Cochrane had taken your blood, you must have realized that the diagnosis of ME was likely to be refuted. Did you decide with your boyfriend that the only way out of the situation was to kill Dr Cochrane and did you persuade him to do the deed?'

For the first time since Sarah had met her, the young woman suddenly seemed to come to life.

'No, that's not true,' she said, her voice high-pitched and louder than Sarah had heard it before. 'I didn't like James, everyone knows that, but I had nothing to do with his death, I swear it, I really didn't.'

The young woman began to rock backwards and forwards, covering her face with her hands, the tears streaming down her face. There was a long silence, with Sarah waiting until she had at last calmed down.

'You're in bad trouble, Amy, and the only way forward is for you to tell me the whole truth about how you got into this situation and then there may be some way of your being able to come to terms with all that's happened and moving forward.'

The young woman stared at Sarah for a few moments and then dropped her gaze.

'All right.'

*

Amy Moffatt's earliest memories of life at home were, when she came to think about it later, rather like the roller-coaster ride her father took her on when she was aged about seven. She was a timid child and during her parents' frequent and spectacular rows, she used to hide in the cupboard under the stairs with her hands over her ears, trying to block out the strident complaints of her mother, often followed by the sound of a blow and high-pitched screams.

There were the bribes when the two of them began to use her as a weapon against each other. Her father fondly believed that she enjoyed the visits when he took her to the various theme parks within reasonable distance, but the carousels and the animals bored her, the roller coasters and the water chutes terrified her and after she had lost control and screamed while on the ghost train, he gave up. As to her mother, she fondly imagined that cream teas and elaborate parties would buy her affection. She was wrong. Always a picky eater and never getting on with other children, she sabotaged the woman's efforts with spectacular attacks of vomiting.

Whatever her parents motives were in adopting David, the result proved to be a disaster all round. Rather than cementing their marriage, it finally destroyed it completely. The two children never got on and after the divorce and her mother's remarriage, if anything the situation became worse. Right from the start she and her half-brother were constantly quarrelling, so much so that James Cochrane, her new stepfather, persuaded her mother that the only possible solution would be to separate the two children as soon as possible.

By that time, Amy was fifteen and they decided to send her to a boarding school, Bristow College. She wasn't bullied there, but what was almost as bad was that she was ignored by the other girls in her house. The teachers, though, and in particular her housemistress, managed to get through to her and she began to settle down.

It was during the summer term of her first year that it happened. She had been sitting just beyond the boundary ropes of the cricket field and, being bored by watching the match, was reading a book in the shade of a large tree when a boy came up to her.

'You're Amy Moffatt, aren't you?'

She tossed her head. 'What if I am?'

The boy smiled. 'Don't be like that, I'm Rupert Mansfield. I've often seen you around, but you're always on your own and I thought you might be lonely.'

Amy was, desperately so, but she wasn't going to admit it and shrugged her shoulders.

'Do you like cricket?'

'No, I think it's boring.'

The boy raised his eyebrows. 'Why are you watching it, then?'

'I'm not, I just wanted to get away from those idiots in my house. All they can find to talk about are boys, fashion and pop music.'

'I can understand fashion and pop music, but as to boys, you've obviously never met the right one and it isn't all about talk, either, you know.'

He sat down beside her and when he just touched the fine hairs on her forearm and then ran it very gently up to her elbow, she gave an involuntary shiver.

'See what I mean?'

It went on from there. He took his time over the next few days, never doing anything to frighten her and when she was still unable to relax, provided the first spliff. After that, she couldn't get enough of it, or him. She got careless, she boasted to the wrong girl, who sneered at her for making it all up and for being a sexless goody-goody.

'That's all you know,' Amy replied.

'Liar.'

'If you go down to the copse after tea on Sunday, you'll see something and might even learn what it's all about.'

Tracy Fairclough was not a nice girl. Not only did she get a view of what was going on, but on another occasion had the additional thrill of watching Miss Richards, to whom she had sent a typewritten note informing her of exactly what the two of them were up to, catching them at it.

'I know that you were both expelled,' Sarah said. 'What happened after that?'

'James gave me an ultimatum. "Either get secretarial training, find a job and make something of your life or you'll be on your own," he said. If it had just been my mother, I would almost certainly have been able to talk her round, but I had long since learned that when James said something, he meant it. I knew that Rupert's father spoiled him silly and my first thought was that the two of us might be able to go somewhere and live together. However, although Mr Mansfield remained indulgent, he was not as indulgent as all that, at least that was what Rupert told me and I never met him.

'Rupert is two years older than me, and at eighteen his father was prepared to get him a job in his City firm, but he would have to learn the ropes properly and show what he was worth, otherwise his allowance would be stopped and there would be no inheritance to look forward to. I knew that Rupert wouldn't be prepared to give all that up and so I had to think of something else.'

'Which was ME, I suppose.'

Amy nodded.

'Tell me about it.'

The idea of overcoming James's bullying about the dreary course in which she had been forced to enrol and the prospect of some awful secretarial job after it, came to Amy suddenly one evening. She had her own TV set in her room at home and one evening saw a programme about ME in which there was a discussion about whether it was a real physical illness or all in the mind. It was that that gave her the idea. She did her homework on the condition on the Internet and the more she read about it the more suitable did it seem for her purpose. She took her time, at first just complaining of fatigue and weakness after her day at the secretarial college and was even able to obtain a letter from the principal saying how unwell she looked and recommending some time off. When she took to her bed and accentuated her natural pallor with suitable make-up, her mother became really anxious and got the GP to make a house call. There was no question of James being involved because he had strong views about treating close relatives.

Amy wasn't going to spoil things by being in too much of a hurry, but when she had downloaded a new article on it and saw the name Audrey Clements as being one of the foremost experts in the field, she really pricked up her ears. The name was vaguely familiar and when she looked her up on the Internet and found that the woman worked at Henshaw Hospital, she suddenly realized where she had heard the name before. She was the psychiatrist with whom James was at daggers drawn and whose name had come up during the conversation that Amy had overheard him having with his daughter, Rebecca, about ME.

It worked out brilliantly. Amy carefully sowed the seed of possible ME in her GP, Dr Holmes's, mind and then told him that she remembered having heard of Dr Clements's name from one of the girls at school, who had the condition and who had done very well under her care. He took the hint, making an appointment for her to see the woman as an out-patient. Her mother, who was convinced that her daughter was gravely ill, took her to the hospital herself in a taxi.

Amy knew that she had won once she had been admitted

for investigation, knowing from her research that there were no tests currently available that would find her out. Had it not been for Dr Clarke, though, she might well not have gone through with it, because she hated Dr Clements from the moment she set eyes on the woman. She knew her type from her experience with the gym mistress at school, but that woman didn't have the licence to examine her intimately, whereas Dr Clements did and took full advantage of it, saying that in view of Amy's sexual experience it was important to rule out any infection; there wasn't even the security of a chaperone to limit the woman's prying fingers.

Dr Clarke was altogether different; she liked him from the start. He always behaved very correctly and later on, when he did domiciliary visits, insisted on Monique being present whenever he saw her in her bedroom. Her mother also liked him, too, and he used to see her afterwards to give her a progress report, which went down particularly well. Amy even began to feel guilty about deceiving the man. As for Cochrane, Amy knew perfectly well that he didn't believe in ME. She had heard him discussing the condition with his daughter, Rebecca, after Sunday lunch a few weeks earlier and she remembered him saying: 'One more article like that and I'll sue the bloody woman for libel.' It was very unusual for him to use language like that and she asked her mother about it the following day.

'Just some row at the hospital, I believe,' she had said, 'I'm sure it will all blow over.'

If Cochrane was upset by her being looked after by one of

his colleagues with whom he was at daggers drawn, he never showed it to her and the longer her illness went on, the less frequently did he come to see her in her room.

Fortunately for her, Cochrane had never seen Rupert Mansfield before, not even a photograph of him, and one Sunday he came to visit her, giving a different name and pretending to be someone she had known at school. Rupert played his part brilliantly. Cochrane was obviously impressed first of all by the way he was dressed. He was wearing a blue jacket, slacks, white shirt and club tie and highly polished brown shoes. Then there were his impeccable manners, his cut-glass accent and his flattering remarks about the house and grounds.

Rupert could be very charming when he tried and that afternoon he laid it on with a trowel. His suggestion that if she wrapped up well, it might do Amy good to be taken for a short drive around Richmond Park was accepted with enthusiasm. If he used the disabled car park, he had added, she might even manage the few steps from there to the attractive pond in the Isabella plantation, where there were seats, so that she would be able to see the flowers and wildlife. That first time, he wasn't going to spoil everything by being away for too long, but even so there was time for a little dalliance in the car, as her mother might have put it.

Gradually, the Sunday afternoon drives lasted longer, they went further afield and they found quiet bits of the Surrey countryside where they were able to take their time, the risk of being discovered by some passing walker adding to their excitement. Inevitably, that wasn't enough and on several Saturday nights when James was away at some meeting or conference, or during his roughly monthly weekend visits to see his mother in the nursing home in Derbyshire, she sneaked out of the house, Rupert picked her up down the road and took her to one of his favourite nightclubs. It was there that she was introduced to cocaine and the high was like nothing she had experienced before, enhancing the pleasures that followed. The fact that she looked terrible the following day did her cause no harm at all, either, and resulted in Monique and her mother fussing over her even more than usual.

It all began to fall apart when Cochrane, accompanied by Monique, came into her room on the Sunday evening after he had got back from the meeting he had been attending. She was still feeling seriously hung over after the excesses of the previous Saturday night and looked with horror at the syringe in its plastic container and the two glass bottles he was carrying.

'Nothing to be frightened about,' he had said briskly. 'As you may know, I have been at a conference for the last couple of days; Dr Clements was also there and we heard a paper about a possible blood test for ME being developed and the author of it asked for samples to be sent to him from known sufferers of the condition so that he can expand his researches. It is early days yet, but he also has ideas about possible treatments. Seeing how much you have suffered, I'm sure you'd welcome the chance to contribute something to furthering knowledge about ME and the possibility of an effective treatment for it.'

Amy was to think later that if she had been less hung over, she might have refused to agree to it, at least until she had asked Dr Clarke for his opinion, but she had only just woken up from a late afternoon sleep, she had a splitting headache and the easiest way to get rid of him was to go along with it. It was all over very quickly and she didn't think too much more about it until Dr Clarke came for his scheduled visit on the Wednesday and asked her about the plaster at the bend of her elbow.

'I see,' he said, a frown on his face, after she had told him what Cochrane had said. 'Very interesting. I hadn't heard about this and I must ask Dr Clements about it when I get back to the hospital.'

Amy didn't think any more about it until the following Sunday when Cochrane was murdered. Her reactions were those of both horror and terror, unable to get the thought out of her head that she might be the next victim. The detailed questioning of the police inspector merely added to her fear and anxiety, as did the arrival of Cochrane's daughter, Rebecca, whom Amy was well aware was, if anything, more cynical about ME than even her father. She just had to get out of the house and it was Rupert, whom she telephoned on her mobile, who told her to get herself admitted to the hospital and well out of the way, also saying that it would be best if they didn't see each other for the time being.

'Have you given any thought to what you're going to do now?' Sarah asked.

'When it's all settled down, Rupert will look after me, I know he will.'

'It seems to me that you are taking all this very lightly. The reality, Amy, is that you're still in trouble, deep trouble, as is he. You've been found to have an illegal drug, cocaine, in your blood. Dr Cochrane had discovered that and you must have thought that his death would solve a lot of the problems. Did you and your boyfriend make the plan to kill him?'

'That's ridiculous.'

'There are those who might not think so and we are in the process of checking Rupert Mansfield's whereabouts at the time Dr Cochrane was murdered. He claims to have been spending the night with a girl he picked up at a disco.'

'He'd never do that, it can't be true, you're making it all up.'

'I'm not, and Mansfield even went as far as to tell me and my colleague that he never wanted to see you again.'

The young woman let out a moan and began to rock backwards and forwards, her head in her hands.

'Now, listen to me,' Sarah said firmly. 'You're well shot of him. Do you really believe that occasional visits to a nightclub and what you got up to at the weekends were ever going to be enough for him? Think about it, and if you do, you'll realize that he's poison for you. Now, you'll remain here under police guard until you are able to go home, which should be within the next day or two. Now, stop making that noise, it isn't going to help anyone, least of all you.'

It was at that moment that Sarah's phone rang; it was Mark Sinclair speaking from the Cochrane's house.

'Just a moment,' she said. 'I'm still with Amy. I'll get the WPC to sit with her while I speak to you outside.'

'Tyrrell's just finished here,' Sinclair said, 'and asked me to give you a call. He's decided that he'd like to bring together all the people who were living in the house at the time of Cochrane's murder, that is Jean Cochrane, Amy, David, the au pair girl, plus his daughter, Rebecca, and Dr Clarke. I don't know exactly what he hopes to achieve by doing so, but he'd like to brief us both tomorrow in his office at the Yard. He also thinks that it might be a good idea to have that meeting on Saturday morning and would like your view about bringing Amy back to the house before the others, perhaps on Friday. What do you think?'

'Amy's not exactly in a great state at the present moment, but maybe the sharp shock I've just given her will be just what's needed. She couldn't possibly manage being in that house alone as soon as tomorrow, though.'

'I agree. I had already thought about that myself and had a word with Monique and her friend, Jess, and they would be prepared to spend just the Friday night at the house with her and it would also allow Monique to collect all her things as she's decided that she doesn't intend to go back to the Cochrane household after that. Mrs Foster would be delighted to have her to continue to stay with them, as is Jess, which I'm quite sure won't surprise you in the least.'

Sarah grinned at the phone. 'You're right, it doesn't.'

Sinclair decided to let that one pass. 'I've also been able to contact the cleaning woman and she is prepared to come tomorrow morning first thing to tidy everything up, and no doubt Monique and Jess will also give her a hand. Mrs Cochrane will come back early on Saturday morning and I have arranged for a car to pick her up; otherwise, I couldn't picture her being organized enough to achieve getting here on time on her own. I've also checked with Rebecca and she is happy, very happy judging by her reaction, to bring David back at the same time. Do you think that Amy's departure tomorrow will be acceptable to the hospital?'

'Not only do I believe that it would be acceptable, but they'll be delighted and it will certainly make my coming interview with Metcalfe that bit easier. I'll break the glad tidings to Amy right away, but just how pleased she is likely to be is a matter of conjecture. I also think it would be wise if I accompanied Amy there with the WPC who's been keeping guard here – we don't want anything to go wrong at the last minute.'

Amy was still snivelling when Sarah went back into the room.

'The good news,' she said, 'is that you'll be able to go back to Roehampton tomorrow. I'll arrange for a car for you and Constable Davies, here, and I will also go with you. You won't be on your own at the house, either. Monique and Jess Foster have agreed to spend the night with you. Your mother will be arriving on Saturday morning, as will David and Rebecca. After that, it will be up to you to get things sorted out, find a job and lead a normal life. No doubt you'll need help and I'm sure you'll be able to find someone to do that.'

Amy began to rock backwards and forwards and let out a

low moan. 'There's no one; my mother would be useless and I hate David. I wish I were dead.'

'What's wrong with David?'

There was a long pause, the young woman covering her face with her hands, then she looked up, tears running down her cheeks. She wiped them away and stared straight at the detective.

'He's a creep. I caught him going through the chest of drawers in my bedroom once when we were in the other house and he told me that my mother needed some sun cream and would he ask me if I had any in my room? It was a lie. I was pretty innocent then and thought he was just trying to see if I had any cash hidden there, because a few weeks earlier a five pound note had gone missing from my purse. In those days, I was very careful with money and I was sure it must have been him who had taken it, although I couldn't prove it. Later on, though, I realized exactly what he was like when Monique told me that she and Jess had caught him spying on them when they were sunbathing topless by the pool. I'm quite sure he was looking for any intimate garments of mine he could find. He's nothing but a filthy pervert as well as a thief and I couldn't live in the same house as him with only my mother there.'

'In that case, why don't you leave? Lots of young women younger than you leave home and find a flat to share with someone. The first thing you need to do is to stop feeling sorry for yourself and accept that you've brought all this on yourself. This is going to be a challenge and that in itself is just what you need. There must be someone you can talk to about it. There is your GP and what about your father? Don't underestimate your mother, either. She has plenty of money and I'm sure she'd help you if you give her a chance. Anyway, all that's something for you to think about later.'

Sarah left the room feeling thoroughly unsettled. Would it have been better to have handled Amy more sympathetically? Should she have arranged for her transfer to a psychiatric unit in another hospital? Suppose the girl killed herself? Was it, as she hoped, the bucket of cold water over the head that the young woman needed? One thing was clear, though, and that was that Amy was an arch manipulator and that was a game Sarah was not prepared to play, not least because the young woman was still a suspect. And what about David? Perhaps Rebecca Cochrane might be able to tell her more about him.

All that was forgotten, at least temporarily, when she was shown into Dr Metcalfe's office and he got up from behind the desk, smiling and holding out his hand.

'I'm very glad to see you,' he said after he had moved his chair round the desk to sit facing her. 'I have been able to put off the meeting of the academic board, but I won't be able to do so much longer. Rumours are flying around and the press are showing an interest as well.'

'We have made quite a lot of progress in our investigation,' Sarah said, 'but we haven't yet been able to pin down the identity of the murderer. We have, though, discovered some disturbing facts about two members of your staff. You know only too well about the ill feeling between Dr Cochrane and Dr Clements and in our view it was most unwise of her to have taken on Amy Moffatt as a patient, even though the initial referral was made by the GP. Amy was after all the daughter of Cochrane's wife and I'm quite sure I don't need to remind you about their dispute over ME and the talk about a possible libel action.

'Now, what really put the cat amongst the pigeons was that Cochrane discovered that Amy hadn't got and never did have ME. Mrs Cochrane's adoptive son, a teenager who also lives in the house, saw Amy leave the house in the small hours of the morning when both Cochrane and Dr Clements were away at a conference at which a possible test for ME was mooted for some time in the near future. It was that that gave Cochrane both the idea and the excuse for testing Amy's blood – he strongly suspected that she had been out on the tiles the previous night. He arranged for the sample to be tested at his daughter's hospital, St Gregory's, and it came back positive for both alcohol and cocaine. We also found a second specimen, which he had left in the fridge in his summerhouse very close to the spot where he was murdered and where he used to work at his hobby of calligraphy. Our tests on that sample confirmed what had been found at St Gregory's and the DNA matched a sample of hair from the girl's brush in her bedroom.

'It was on the following Sunday morning that Cochrane was murdered but we don't believe that either Dr Clements or Dr Clarke killed him. Dr Clements has a cast-iron alibi and we don't consider it likely that Dr Clarke was responsible, although we haven't eliminated him entirely from our inquiries. However, we did discover some very disturbing details about the way they were both handling Amy's case. Firstly, we gather that one of the nurses looking after her during her initial admission found her in a very distressed state after Dr Clements had examined her on her own without a chaperone. The nurse was concerned that the examination had been of an unnecessarily intimate nature and she consulted one of the doctors working on the ward. Amy confirmed to me what had been suspected, but had no wish to take the matter further either at that time or now. After much heart searching, the doctor decided that unless Amy herself changed her mind, there was nothing further to be done about it and, understandably has no wish to be involved so long after the event. Under these circumstances, there is no way that this matter can be pursued any further by us.

'As for Dr Clarke, he admits to having had an inappropriate relationship with Amy's mother, Cochrane's wife, while doing his domiciliary visits to see Amy. However, we are quite satisfied that as far as the young woman is concerned, he behaved with perfect propriety. How can we be so certain about all this? Cochrane obviously suspected that something was going on and had put listening devices in both Amy's and his wife's bedrooms, the recordings of which we have heard.'

The man facing Sarah shook his head wearily. 'So, from the way you put it, it sounds as if neither the girl, Amy, nor her mother are likely to make formal complaints about those members of our staff that you've just mentioned.'

'That's right. Amy, as you may imagine, is in a very fragile state just now and she's going to find it very difficult to come to terms with what has happened as it is. She has been caught out in a major deception, her boyfriend has ditched her, and I can't see her being prepared to face the inevitable publicity if she were to make a formal complaint about Dr Clements. As for Mrs Cochrane, as judged by the recordings that her husband, Dr Cochrane, made, it is quite clear that she cooperated freely with everything that went on between her and Dr Clarke and her embarrassment would certainly be profound if the press got hold of it, not to mention the disastrous effect it would have on his career.'

'What's going to happen to the girl, Amy, in the immediate future?' Metcalfe asked.

'I'm pleased to be able to tell you that I've just heard that our investigations at Cochrane's house have been completed and Amy will be able to return home tomorrow and I will arrange for transport and an escort. We propose to keep up the guard on her room here until she leaves. As I am sure you realize, she is still in a fragile mental state and we don't want to risk her running away before her mother is able to take responsibility for her.'

Metcalfe nodded his head slowly. 'I can't tell you how pleased I am to hear what you have told me about the girl. I am sure you must be aware that there has been a considerable clamour generated here by this whole business, with all sorts of rumours floating about, and the longer it goes on the more damaging it's likely to get. However, getting her away from here will undoubtedly calm things down and take some of the pressure off. I'll have to speak to the chairman of the hospital's board of governors to tell him about this development and I'm sure he'll be pleased, too. As for Doctors Clements and Clarke, that's another horror that will have to be tackled, quite possibly also by the board. At least we are still one of the very few NHS and university hospitals to have one.'

CHAPTER NINE

JACK POCOCK WAS waiting for them outside the house in Roehampton when Tyrrell and Sinclair arrived that afternoon.

'I suggest that we look round outside first, sir, and follow the route that Mr Howarth, the man who found Cochrane's body, used. He had seen his neighbour lying with his head in the goldfish pond, from his side of the fence, which separates the two properties. The front door was locked, but he managed to rouse the boy, who told him from his bedroom window that that door between the house and the garage was not secured and that he would be able to get into the garden that way. That's the one there, sir.'

'So, the boy didn't come down himself?'

'No, sir, he didn't and knowing how emotional Mrs Cochrane could be, Mr Howarth, having already seen that Dr Cochrane was clearly dead, thought it best not to involve the boy any further and to deal with the situation himself.'

They followed the route Howarth had taken and at each stage Pocock showed them the photographs that had been taken.

'That indent there is where the stone that killed Dr Cochrane was lifted; it must have been thrown over that fence over there, because we found it in the neighbour's garden. There was Cochrane's blood on it, but no other DNA and it's possible that the murderer was wearing gloves, although we found no trace of any fibres on the stone nor contaminated gloves, either in the grounds, garage or house.'

'Do you think that a woman would have been able to inflict the injury to Cochrane?' Tyrrell asked Mark Sinclair.

'There's no doubt about that. Tredgold showed us a video of the very stone being wielded by one of his female assistants on a skull that he had obtained from a medical school anatomy department. The young woman was slightly built, but she was able to deliver one blow with sufficient force to cause a depressed fracture of that skull, not dissimilar to the one that occurred in Cochrane's case.'

Tyrrell raised his eyebrows. 'A somewhat macabre experiment, I must say, but it appears to have proved the point.'

After inspecting the goldfish pond and the photographs of the victim lying face down with his face in the water, they moved into the hut where they were shown the refrigerator in which the sample of Amy's blood had been found and some of Cochrane's designs, which were still lying on the table.

On their way back past the swimming pool, Pocock pointed out the exact spot where David Moffatt must have been standing when he took the photographs of the two semi-naked girls sunbathing and involving themselves in a variety of other activities.

'How come you were able to pinpoint it so accurately, Jack?' Tyrrell asked.

'We took some pictures of two WPC's of roughly the same build and positioned in the same place, sir.'

'Not naked, I trust?'

Pocock gave an audible sigh. 'No, sir.'

'Glad to hear it.'

'How did you get hold of the boy's pictures?'

'He had transferred them from the flash card on his camera to his computer and then put them on a file with a password. The boy clearly has an interest in the subject because he had downloaded a number of other images of the same type from various websites, and we also have copies of those.'

'Did you remove them from his computer completely?'

'No, sir. I thought that they might be needed as evidence and decided to leave that decision to you. The computer is back in the boy's room.'

'Will he know what you've done?'

'I think it very unlikely.'

'You were quite right to do all that and I think they're best left where they are for the time being. We don't want the boy alerted if, by any chance, he was involved in Cochrane's murder. If that's everything out here, Jack, perhaps you'd show us the interior of the house.'

Pocock took them into every room inside, starting with Cochrane's study, showing them the locked filing cabinet, in which the man had kept his personal documents, the correspondence with the school over Amy's expulsion, those with the Medical Defence Union and his solicitor over his dispute with Dr Clements and finally his will.'

'Mark, you know about that, don't you?'

'Yes, sir, I went over it with one of our legal experts. Cochrane's left the house and contents to his wife and she will get the NHS death benefit and the proceeds of his life insurance. He did have some reasonably substantial investments and the income from some of that is in a trust to be used for the boy David's further education. When that is over, the residue will go to his natural daughter, Rebecca.'

'Any comment on that, Mark?'

'Rebecca told Sarah that with her NHS salary, and also having inherited her mother's estate, she's already comfortably off and is quite happy with the arrangements that her father had made.'

'I see. Who are the trustees of the education monies for David?'

'Rebecca, Walter Paterson, a close friend, who works at Henshaw Hospital as a clinical neurophysiologist, whom we've met, and his solicitor. We've only just discovered that Cochrane's mother is still alive and is in a nursing home in Derbyshire. That is also being financed by a trust, administered by a firm of solicitors. Cochrane's father was very wealthy and I gather that the income and further capital from his estate is sufficient to make her position secure for the rest of her life. The residue on her death will go to various charities. She is already in her eighties and is not expected to live much longer. There is no evidence of any recent alterations or of Cochrane having made a new will.'

Upstairs, Pocock showed them all the rooms, paying particular attention to the bugging devices in Amy's bedroom and that of her mother, and David Moffatt's computer in his.

'The boy clearly has a particular interest in naked girls, as I already said, and he had several files of them on passwords, which is why it took quite some time to gain access to them. They contain colour photographs and some short film clips downloaded from various sites on the Internet showing them indulging in a variety of activities. There were also a lot of images of the au pair girl and her friend in and around the pool, which came from his still and video camera and from which we made prints, and I have copies in my briefcase here.'

'Hmm,' Tyrrell said when he had looked at them. 'No wonder that young woman threw him into the pool, and what do you suppose she might have done had she known about these? Presumably, David Moffatt thinks they are safe behind his passwords. I think you were quite right, Jack, not to have deleted them permanently.'

'While we're in here, sir,' Pocock said, pointing to the window in the boy's room, 'If you look out, you'll be able to see that it is almost directly above the front door and one does get a good view of anyone walking along the path towards the gate and the street. I arranged for one of the female SOCOs to do just that after dusk and she was clearly visible.'

'Any street lights in the vicinity, Jack?'

'None close enough to make any difference.'

'Anything else?'

'Yes, sir. If you take a look at the side of the wardrobe over there, you'll see a wooden pole with a metal hook at the end which fits the catch on the trapdoor.'

Pocock took it outside and pulled the door down and, as it opened, a light came on in the loft above and they saw the aluminium ladder above.

'That particular light is on a timer, but the other lights and the power for the model railway have separate switches up there. These ladders are usually in sections which can be locked into place as you pull them down, but this one is made in one piece and there is sufficient height in the loft for it to be manoeuvred up and down along guides, so that once anyone is up there it can be pulled up and the handle on the inner surface of the hatch allows it to be closed from inside.'

'So the boy would have been able to spend time up there with complete privacy?'

'Yes, sir. There is also ventilation and heating in the loft as well.'

'All that must have cost a bit.'

Pocock nodded. 'If you'd all care to take a look, sir, I'll go up first and turn on the main lighting and the power for the set.'

The loft area was very large indeed and the models had been set out on a series of trestle tables linked together, set on the boarded floor, leaving a central area free, which allowed access to the various scenes set around it. There were two separate railway systems. The express, which was able to travel between two stations, wound its way through a tunnel, over a bridge and around the perimeter of the circuit past a level crossing, at which were waiting lines of vehicles on each side. There were signals and on the platforms of each station were railway officials, waiting passengers and taxis on the road outside. The track of the country train was directed on a separate and more complicated route, passing through fields with sheep and cattle on them, there were a number of level crossings on it, with waiting cars and farm vehicles there and also on the approach roads. There was also CD player and Pocock played a few of snatches of railway sounds, those of a steam train, blasts on whistles, countryside sounds and announcements.

Each system had a separate control panel fitted with a joystick, which controlled the speed and direction of each train and the three detectives each had a turn on it.

'This takes me back,' Tyrrell said, 'although I never had a set-up to touch this when I was a child. These days I imagine this sort of thing is usually in the hands of some obsessive older man, reliving his past. I can't see most modern children having the patience or the interest both to collect and spend time on it. I wonder if Cochrane enjoyed having a go on it himself.'

'I doubt it somehow,' said Sinclair, 'he was a busy psychiatrist and, as you've already seen, he had hobbies of his own. From what I've heard about David, though, I can well imagine him becoming obsessed by it and spending hours up here.'

'But why do you suppose it was shut down? Any views, Mark?'

'I wonder if it was a punishment devised by Cochrane when

he discovered what David had been doing with his camera. Monique's girlfriend told us that she had had a word with the man about the boy's behaviour at the swimming pool.'

'That makes sense. How exactly had the shut-down process been achieved, Jack?'

'The automatic light, which comes on when the hatch is lowered is on a timer, the rest of the lights and the power for the trains are controlled by that junction box with a panel of switches attached to it. The former, which is powered by a low-wattage bulb was working when I first went up here, but the junction box had been capped, I'm almost certain by a professional electrician. We certainly needed one to reconnect it.'

'That, undoubtedly points to Cochrane being responsible for organizing it,' Tyrell said. Have the two of you finished checking the alibis of Amy's boyfriend and those at the hospital who had reason to dislike, or even hate, Cochrane?'

'Yes, sir,' Sinclair replied. 'Dr Clements seems to be in the clear with regard to Cochrane's death. She was in bed all that night and early morning with her female partner, or whatever other euphemism one wants to use these days. The latter has become disenchanted with the liaison and the way she was being treated and we were convinced that she was telling us the truth. She also made it very clear what a thoroughly unpleasant person Dr Clements is. She is also in serious trouble, not only over the ME question and her possible libel of James Cochrane. It appears that she carried out an intimate and inappropriate examination on Amy when she was first admitted to hospital, and as well as the girl herself there are two others who might be prepared to corroborate it, although they have their own careers to think about and I doubt if they would, even if push came to shove. Sarah, who has seen more of Amy than anyone else, also thinks it very unlikely that she would want to complain about it now.

'By using a bug in her bedroom, Cochrane recorded the senior registrar, Dr Clarke, having sex with his wife, Jean, after the man had seen Amy. Clarke claims to have been asleep in his flat at the time of the murder, but there was no one else there able to confirm that. He lives alone, says that he hasn't had a regular girlfriend since he and his wife divorced eighteen months ago and claims not to have recovered fully from that yet. As you know, sir, we have interviewed him at length in the presence of his solicitor and we believe that what he told us was true.

'As for Amy's old school friend, Rupert Mansfield, we interviewed him together and found him to be a thoroughly nasty piece of work. He was quite happy to dump Amy once the going got tough and claims to have been with a girl he picked up at a club the evening before Cochrane's murder and to have spent the whole night with her. We have arranged for a detective constable to make enquiries at the club, but neither of us is optimistic about a positive result.

'That leaves the people in this house, Jean Cochrane, Amy, the au pair girl and David. All of them, except Monique, had various reasons for disliking if not hating Cochrane and all of them knew about his early Sunday morning habits. There is no direct incriminating evidence against any of them.'

'What about the man who found the body and rang for the ambulance? You've no doubt interviewed him?'

'Yes, his name is Howarth and I did have a word with him and ran some checks on him as well and I think we can rule him out. Considering the degree of disability he has as the result of severe arthritis of both hips – he has had them replaced on both sides and neither operation has been particularly successful – he did remarkably well to get to Cochrane so quickly. He used to be a regular soldier, served in Northern Ireland, and reacted calmly and effectively as he looked over the wall and saw the man lying in the pond. Before leaving his house, he called for an ambulance, then got his car out, drove round, entered the garden by the door between the garage and the house and as soon as he found that Cochrane was dead with his head in the pond, he called the police.'

'So the murderer could have got into the garden the same way as the neighbour?'

'It's certainly a possibility, but I've had a word with all the people living in close proximity to the house and none of them heard anything untoward that morning or saw a car drawing up near the house until Howarth arrived. One woman, who is an early morning dog walker, also told us that there were no strange cars drawn up on either side of the road between the gate to the park and her house, which is several hundred yards beyond the Cochrane property.'

'Thank you, and you, Jack. All that I have seen and heard makes the whole business much clearer to me. I have to report to the Commissioner on Monday and, as that fellow who's on the Henshaw Hospital Board and who approached us in the first place is still making my superior colleague's life a misery, I think it essential that I meet all those who were present here at the time of the murder and see how they interact. I think that we should leave Dr Clements out of it for the time being as her alibi seems to be quite solid. Perhaps the simplest way to do that would be to get them altogether, if possible on Saturday morning and see what follows from that. Do you think that would be possible, Mark?'

'I don't see why not, sir. May I suggest that Sarah conducts the meeting? She knows Amy and Mrs Cochrane much better than I do.'

'I agree. Tell her to give me a ring if she has any reservations.'

During the journey in the car back to her flat with David, Rebecca Cochrane was already beginning to think that she might have made a terrible mistake. All her attempts at conversation had been met at best by monosyllabic replies and at worst with complete silence and the boy sat bolt upright, staring through the windscreen without ever once turning his head in her direction. Gradually, though, when they were in the flat, once he had unpacked, slotted the compact disc that the policeman had given him into her laptop and satisfied himself that all the data he required was retrievable, he began to relax, getting down to work once they had had lunch.

It was in the late morning of the Friday afternoon of that

week and Rebecca was doing some much needed housework when the front door bell rang. She opened it to see the female detective inspector standing there.

'I'm sorry to disturb you, but rather than phoning I thought I'd come round and explain what we are planning for tomorrow.'

'Come in. The place is rather a mess, I'm afraid.'

'Any chance of coming out with me for a quick bite of lunch?'

Rebecca Cochrane smiled. 'What a good idea! David's got his last exam this afternoon and I won't have to leave here to pick him up at school before about half past four. It's not the greatest time for traffic, but at least I won't have to do it again.'

Rebecca had liked what little she had seen of the detective and once they were seated opposite each other in the small Italian restaurant only a few hundred yards away, conversation came quite easily.

'To be honest,' she said, 'I regretted my decision to bring David to my flat as soon as we got into the car. Why did I do it, then? I think it was because I felt sorry for him. You see, Jean and her first husband should never have adopted him in the first place. I think they only did it because they were having problems with Amy and must have thought that a brother would be just what she needed. It's not being unfair to say that Jean is no intellectual and that she lives by her emotions and the trashy "light love" novels she is so fond of reading. I have no idea what part Malcolm Moffatt played in all this; I've never met him and under the circumstances it would have been the height of tactlessness for my even bringing up his name with anyone at the house in Roehampton.

'David must have been deeply upset by my father's death and the fact that he doesn't show it doesn't surprise me in the least. I suspect that displaying emotion of any sort was squeezed out of him in a succession of care homes.'

'How about his relationship with Amy?'

'They were always like chalk and cheese. He's all intellect and no emotion and she's the exact opposite. He's the one who blew the whistle on her to my father, and to put no finer point on it, they hate each other. Amy gets all Jean's attention and now that Dad's gone, David must feel that he's entirely on his own. Having said that, though, he's not the easiest person to love as he's so self-contained.

'I know perfectly well that people think I am tarred with the same brush and there is a good deal of truth in that. However, I like to think that I'm perfectly capable of recognizing the need for it in others and, even though I say it myself, I believe my detachment and lack of emotion have helped me to handle my patients sympathetically, but without personal involvement.

'Over the last few days, I have thought a good deal about my father and those close to him. Many's been the time that I've wondered why he married Jean and I think I know the answer to that one now. I was an observant child and early in my adolescence I became aware that he liked to look at the pretty girls on the beach and even on the streets with a good deal more than casual attention. I knew about sex; how could

I not when it was the main focus of interest for quite a few of the girls in my boarding school? However, that wasn't true of me; schoolwork and games were what I really enjoyed and close and clinging friendships with the other girls weren't for me either. I also came to understand that I was very much my mother's daughter. She was a loving parent to me and a cheerful, outgoing woman, who had many interests and a large circle of mainly female friends, but that was it. I'm quite sure that sex for her had been part of the marriage contract and that although she went along with it cheerfully enough, it hadn't mattered to her any more than that. Why was I so sure? The answer to that is quite simple and that is that I am like that myself. That's not to say that I don't have impulses in that direction, but I'm perfectly happy to deal with them in my own way.

'My father was quite different, being a very tactile man, but he also had very firm views about honour and I'm quite sure that he wouldn't have strayed while married to my mother. After her death, though, he had been ripe for the picking and that was when he met Jean. Although I have to admit that I believe Jean to be a profoundly silly woman with pretensions of being "to the manor born" and no great beauty, she certainly has a strong sexual aura. Perhaps the explanation might lie in pheromones. Whatever the reason, I'm quite sure that Jean was and is up to it in bed and, for that matter, out of it as well, She has an aura about her, all right; one only has to see how men look at her to understand how strong her attraction is to them in that way. I also believe that she will come out of the present situation perfectly all right; she is going to be wealthy, another man will respond to her and that will be that. Would Jean have wanted to kill my father? The very idea is ridiculous.

'What about Amy? She is undoubtedly a manipulative, devious little slut, but a violent murderess? I think that is wildly unlikely, although she will no doubt continue to run rings round her mother and get her own way. As to David, there can be no denying that he is spooky in his obsessive way, but is he violent? Surely not. With the provisions my father has made for him in his will, I can see him finishing up as a boffin, perhaps in the field of computers. My father did tell me about his spying on Monique and her friend while they were swimming and sunbathing and that he was very concerned about the boy in that regard.

'"Don't worry, Dad," I said to him. "Lots of boys of that age are like that; it doesn't mean anything and I'm sure he'll grow out of it."'

'Once the dust has settled, how do you see yourself in relation to the family?' Sarah asked.

'It may sound selfish and I suppose it is, but I have my career and personal life to think about. I took David in for these few days because I felt sorry for him, but there's no point in mincing words, I want nothing to do with any of them again once my father's affairs are settled.'

'Have you had any ideas at all why someone would want to kill your father?' Sarah asked.

'Believe me, I've thought of little else since it happened and although of course I realize that there were serious tensions affecting him at both places, I just can't see anyone at the hospital or at home even contemplating doing that. A damaged patient would be my best guess, although I realize that that's a considerable rarity. You see, Dad was such a quiet man, some might have said rather dull, and I can't see an even half-normal person having even considered killing him.'

'There's something been worrying me about entry to the garden the morning your father was killed,' Sarah said. 'I think you said you didn't know what he did about the gate between the house and the garage when the family were in residence. Do you think he would have bolted it last thing at night?'

'I think it quite likely. Dad was a very careful and in some ways obsessional man.'

'Do you suppose he would have opened it before going to the summerhouse the morning he was killed?'

'I don't know, but I rather doubt it. I can't see any point in his doing so.'

Sarah nodded. 'How's David been these last few days?'

'No trouble at all to me personally, but I have been concerned about the amount of time he's spent beavering away with his books and the computer. I had a mind to tell him when he first came here that with only two days to go before his exams he'd be better off relaxing, but decided not to give in to the temptation. I haven't been in medicine for four years without knowing that obsessionals aren't amenable to reason and so I've just let him get on with it. Over breakfast and in the evenings he's said almost nothing to me. We have watched the odd TV programme together after supper, but for the most part he was either studying one of his textbooks or working on the laptop.'

'Everything is more or less settled at the house in Roehampton, so would you be able to bring David over on Saturday morning? I'll give you a ring to confirm the time. Chief Superintendent Tyrrell, who is in overall charge of the investigation, will be there and he would like to meet everyone to bring them up to date with our enquiries so far.'

'Does that include me.'

'Of course.'

Rebecca had enjoyed meeting Sarah Prescott, liking her cheerful manner and it had been a relief to air her thoughts and concerns with someone of her own age and gender. After lunch, they had been for a walk in the nearby Bishop's Palace Garden and she was able to relax and chat about this and that, anything, in fact, other than the recent events that has upset so many people, not least herself.

Rebecca picked David up from the school late that afternoon and he was his usual taciturn self, hardly saying anything either at supper or afterwards. She woke on the Saturday morning feeling more cheerful than she had done since hearing the dreadful news of her father's death. For the first time since David had come to stay, she was up before him; hardly surprising, she thought, as after the stress of the exams he no doubt needed a lie-in. However, after her shower and when she was in the kitchen setting out the crockery, cereal, yoghourt and fruit, she heard him moving into the bathroom. He appeared just as she had finished boiling her egg – he had refused the offer of one on his first morning with her, saying that he only ever had cereal and toast at home.

'Good morning, David,' she said as he came into the room and sat down. 'I hope you had a good sleep?' she asked.

'Yes, thank you.' There was a long pause. 'Do I really have to go back to be with Jean?'

'Yes, you do, David. We've already been over the whole business at length and it's been agreed with her. I've got to return to work on Monday and it's just not possible for you to stay here any longer. Now, I've promised to get you there no later than eleven, so you'd better start getting ready. Don't forget anything, particularly that CD in my computer with your work on it. Would you also strip your bed, please, and put the sheets and pillow cases in the basket in the bathroom?'

Rebecca was both obsessional and very much a creature of habit. She always put the weekly wash on every Saturday morning and after she had cleared up in the kitchen, took the dirty clothes basket from the bathroom into her bedroom and emptied the contents on to the floor, adding her pyjamas and the sheets and pillow cases from her bed. It was when she was sorting through the pile that she noticed it. There should have been seven pairs of panties and there were only six. She had twelve pairs altogether, she was wearing the one that she had put on that morning after her shower and there were four clean ones in her chest of drawers. She was already pretty sure about it, but she checked the corridor and the bathroom, to make sure that she hadn't dropped one, and also went through the pile of sheets and clothes again. There could be no doubt about it, there was one missing.

'The dirty little tick,' she said to herself.

What should she do about it? By the time she had loaded the washing machine, she had decided not to confront David in the flat. She hadn't heard that he had ever given in to any form of violent behaviour, but she wasn't prepared to gamble on it. There were plenty of knives in the kitchen and with all the fuss in the media about them, one would have had to be both deaf and blind not to know that teenagers were quite capable of using them.

To her considerable relief, David got into the car on time and without trying again to persuade her to let him stay with her, and throughout the journey he didn't say a word. The good-looking male detective appeared at the front door as they walked up the path towards the house in Roehampton.

'Hello, David,' he said, also smiling in Rebecca's direction. 'How did the exams go?'

'Not too badly, thank you.'

'Good, the others are waiting in the sitting-room, so that we will be able to give you all an update on how things are proceeding with our inquiries. Why not leave your case in the hall and go on in and find a seat?'

Sarah Prescott was also standing nearby and Rebecca signalled to her as Sinclair and David went through the door to the sitting-room. Quickly, she told the young woman about the missing piece of underwear. David's case wasn't locked and it was the work of only a couple of minutes for them to go through the contents and there was no sign of it.

'I'm quite sure that he took it; they must be in his trouser pocket – they're quite flimsy.'

'Don't worry, I promise I'll deal with it later on. Why not join the others?'

CHAPTER TEN

THE THREE DETECTIVES, accompanied by the large bulk of Sergeant Bristow, had arrived at the Cochrane house soon after nine that morning and they were let in by Jessica Foster.

'Monique is making sure that Amy is presentable and she should be down within a few minutes,' the young woman said after Sarah had made the introductions.

'Surely not breakfast in bed?' Sinclair asked, raising his eyebrows slightly.

The young woman smiled. 'No fear, but having her bath and getting dressed before coming down was more than enough for her on her first morning here and we had no intention of taking it up to her in her room. She can get it herself later if she's feeling peckish.'

'Good for you. I always think that starting as you mean to go on is the best policy in situations like this.'

'Do feel free to leave as soon as Amy's ready,' Tyrrell said. 'We're most grateful for your help, but we don't wish to impose on you and Monique.'

'That's all right. I know that Monique would like to say a

proper goodbye to Mrs Cochrane; after all she has been here for nearly a year and she has grown quite fond of her. There is also David!' The young woman raised her eyebrows slightly, 'I'm sure Monique wouldn't want to leave him out, either. Why don't you go into the sitting-room and I'll let you know when Amy's ready to come down? After that, I'll be in Monique's room, helping her to pack and check that nothing's been left behind, and you'll be able to contact me there when the time comes.'

'Sarah,' Tyrrell said, when Jessica had left them on their own, 'you're the one who has seen most of Amy and her mother and I gather that Mark has already told you that I think it would be best if you were to conduct the session when the Cochrane family are all here. It looks as if they won't be arriving much before eleven and that will give us ample time to decide both the best way to handle matters and also to see how Amy's settled back here. Are you happy about that?'

'Yes, sir. I'll do my best.'

Tyrrell smiled. 'I know you will.'

'Any other points, Mark?'

'While you're getting an impression of what Mrs Cochrane and Amy are like, why don't I show Sarah the one thing that she's missed up to now and that's David's railway set-up in the loft. It'll also give her more insight into his character.'

Tyrrell smiled. 'Good idea, but don't tell me that you're not looking forward to having another go with those trains.'

'Touché.'

After Sarah had arranged for Monique to bring both Amy and Jean Cochrane down to the drawing-room to meet Tyrrell,

Sinclair took the pole from David's bedroom, pulled down the ladder, climbed up and disappeared inside the loft. He switched on the main power, then let out a low whistle as he looked round.

'Come on up, Sarah, and I'll give you a hand with the last bit.'

They stayed up there for a good ten minutes and then went back down, put the pole back where they had found it and returned to the sitting-room.

Tyrrell had a son and two daughters in their early twenties and late teens and it was obvious that he had managed to get on to Amy's wavelength with no great trouble. She was actually smiling at something he had just said as they went in through the door. He was clearly equally adept at dealing with Mrs Cochrane, who was sitting beside her daughter on the sofa.

'I wonder if I might have a quick word with you, sir?' Sarah said as she went into the room and then made a gesture with her mobile phone in her hand. 'Something's just come up and I'd like your advice.'

The two of them left the room and went into Cochrane's study where Sarah told him what they had found in the loft. For the next five minutes, Tyrrell listened carefully to what she had to say and how she proposed to handle it and, after making comments himself and thinking about it carefully, said:

'Right, I agree that that would be the best way to handle everybody and I'll brief Reg Bristow before you start.'

It was a considerable relief to Sinclair when Tyrrell and

Sarah returned, as after their departure the two women kept silent, casting anxious looks in his direction.

'Sorry about that,' Tyrrell said, smiling at the two women. 'That phone call took quite a bit longer to deal with than I had expected, but it's all sorted now. Amy, you were telling me about that friend of yours from school, who's a model, and were wondering about getting into that yourself. It's not easy to break into it, as I'm sure you know, but....'

To Sarah's surprise, Tyrrell seemed to know a good deal about the fashion business, the names of models, photographers and couturiers tripping off his tongue, and Amy even became quite animated, some colour appearing in her cheeks.

It was nearly eleven by the time that David, Rebecca Cochrane and Andrew Clarke had arrived and after Monique and Jessica had left, having said their goodbyes, Tyrrell gestured towards the various chairs, which had been augmented by several from the dining-room, scattered around the drawing-room. Jean Cochrane was on the sofa with Amy by her side, Rebecca Cochrane in an easy chair to one side of it and Andrew Clarke on the other, while the three detectives were on the dining-room chairs facing them and David perched on the piano stool, peering across the room through his thick-lensed glasses despite being offered a fourth chair, and Sergeant Bristow stood stolidly by the door.

'As you will know already,' Tyrrell said, after he had formally introduced himself to Rebecca, David and Andrew Clarke, 'we were called in to inquire into Dr Cochrane's murder after your neighbour, Mr Howarth, who lives in the house directly behind this one, saw him lying with his head partly in the goldfish pond early on the morning of the Sunday before last. The investigation has been carried out by our specialist team directed by my two assistants here, Inspectors Prescott and Sinclair, and the former will take us through all that has been discovered.' Tyrrell made a gesture towards Sarah. 'Inspector Prescott!'

'Thank you, sir. It became clear following the pathologist's report that Dr Cochrane must have been kneeling by the pond feeding the goldfish, as he always did early on Sunday mornings, when he was struck a severe blow on the back of his head. It was delivered by a large stone, which had been lifted from the undergrowth near the side path and later thrown over the fence into the neighbouring garden, where our forensic team found it. The impact was severe enough to have fractured his skull and rendered him unconscious; he pitched forward into the pond and his death was due to drowning. Within the following hour he was seen by Mr Howarth, who was working in his garden and wanted to ask Dr Cochrane about the pollarding of some trees overhanging the fence. The man immediately rang for an ambulance and when he came round in his car and went into the garden to see if there was anything he could do, he discovered that Dr Cochrane was already dead and it was then that he called the police.

'David was already awake and when the man hammered on the front door, he leaned out of his bedroom window and, after telling him that he would be able to get into the back garden through the door between the garage and the house, he said that he would inform his mother about what had happened.

'It is clear that whoever murdered Dr Cochrane must have known about his usual Sunday morning routine when he was at home, which was to get up early, have his breakfast, then walk along the side path to the summerhouse, unlock it, collect the fish food and, after he had finished sprinkling it on the water, return to the summerhouse to work on his designs. His assailant, who had followed him along the path, picked up the large stone from the undergrowth nearby and hit him with it as he was kneeling by the pond.

'The forensic scientists have determined that although heavy, the stone could have been lifted by a woman as well as a comparatively slight man, indeed by any one of those living in this house, Mrs Cochrane, Amy, Monique and David. Clearly, too, it would have been possible for someone from outside, such as Dr Clarke, to enter the garden by the unlocked door I mentioned earlier, or indeed from one of the neighbours' properties over the various fences. However, after having inspected the gardens on both sides, the one behind and all the fences, our specialist team found no evidence of that and were able to rule that possibility out.

'Now, there were a number of people who had reason to dislike or even hate Dr Cochrane and would have been happy to see him out of the way. There was Dr Clements, a colleague at Henshaw Hospital, who is obsessed with the idea of ME being a purely physical illness and who had written a letter to one of the medical journals decrying Dr Cochrane's reservations about that and which, in the opinion of Dr Cochrane's solicitor, was libellous. She had invested a great deal in Amy's case as a severe example of the physical nature of the illness. She must have known, too, from Dr Clarke, who did the domiciliary visits to Amy and noticed the plaster at the bend of her elbow, that Dr Cochrane had himself taken a blood sample from Amy. Did Dr Clements put two and two together and realize that if he had proved that Amy had been on drugs, her diagnosis would be very much put in doubt and her clinical judgement would also be questioned. That would be a very serious matter for her and, as a result, did she decide to kill him before her standing and even her career in psychiatry were damaged irreparably?

'Although Dr Cochrane's death would undoubtedly have taken a load off her shoulders, we didn't think that she would have gone to such lengths. She wouldn't have known that the blood test showed that Amy had been taking cocaine and alcohol and she has a reliable alibi herself for early that Sunday morning. Did she, though, get her assistant, Dr Clarke, to kill Cochrane for her? As a result of his many domiciliary visits, he knew the layout of the house and had met all those living here. Did Dr Clements know that he was having a physical relationship with Dr Cochrane's wife and thus was able to blackmail him into doing the deed for her?'

Sarah glanced at the people in the room and saw that Jean Cochrane had turned pale, looking as if she was about to faint, that Amy was sitting bolt upright and staring straight ahead, her tension being apparent from the tightness of her neck muscles, while Andrew Clarke kept his gaze firmly fixed on the floor in front of him.

'If Dr Clements didn't know what you and Dr Clarke were

doing together after his visits to Amy,' Sarah said, looking directly at the Jean Cochrane, 'your husband most certainly did. You see, he must have had strong enough suspicions to have put a sophisticated listening device in your bedroom, from which he was able to make recordings. Did you decide to kill your husband, Mrs Cochrane, or did you and Dr Clarke decide to do it together? He says he was asleep in his flat at the time of the murder, but there is no one to confirm that and both he and you would have had plenty of time to get back into the house and he to return to his flat before the body was discovered.

'And what about you, Amy? Most people would have considered you physically far too weak to have killed Dr Cochrane in the way it was done. We know, though, that you never had ME and were using the pretence of it to avoid having to work and were enjoying yourself with your boyfriend at weekends and on nights out in London whenever Dr Cochrane was away visiting his mother. You pretended that the young man who took you out for drives bored you and that you didn't enjoy his visits, while Dr Cochrane, who liked his formal appearance and good manners, never suspected that he was none other than the same young man who had been expelled from school with you for drug taking and sex. No wonder, after what you got up to during those afternoons out, you looked exhausted when you got back.

'Dr Cochrane certainly suspected that you were faking your illness, though, and after you were seen sneaking out of the house during the night when he was away at a conference, he took a blood sample from you and was able to show that you had taken both cocaine and alcohol during that time, probably on the Saturday night, by getting the specimen analyzed at his daughter's hospital. He had also left a second specimen in the refrigerator in the summerhouse and that enabled us to confirm his findings.'

Sarah saw Amy staring at David with a look of utter loathing, but he didn't turn away, tilting his head slightly and with a hint of a smirk on his face.

'Now, we mustn't forget you, David, must we? You knew that like you, Dr Cochrane, was a very careful man and one of his obsessional habits was always to feed the goldfish before starting his calligraphy in the summerhouse; perhaps he even told you about it. You also knew that at that early hour no one else would be about and no doubt you had moments of anxiety when Mr Howarth knocked on the front door, realizing that had he happened to look over the fence earlier, he might have seen what you had done.

'In a way, the man finding Dr Cochrane so early might even have been a relief for you, as otherwise he might have remained lying with his head in the pond for hours, if not the whole day, unless the two young women had decided to have a swim. Howarth would confirm that you were up in your bedroom when he arrived fairly soon after the murder and you thought that no one would suspect you. You weren't to know that we would find out about Dr Cochrane's obsessional habits and how careful he was about bolting the door between the garage and the house on the inside every evening before he went to bed. Did he forget to bolt it the previous evening or did he unbolt it before going to the summerhouse that Sunday morning? It would have been out of character for him to have done the first and the second possibility doesn't seem to me to be very likely, there being no very obvious reason for his doing so.

'However, the opposite was true in your case. Did you unbolt it before, or more likely after, you had killed Dr Cochrane, to make it look as if someone might have come in from outside to carry out the murder? I think you did. Why did you kill him? You're a voyeur as well as a murderer, aren't you, David? I'm quite sure you know exactly what that means. You spied on Monique and her friend, Jess, when they were at the swimming pool, but you did more than that, didn't you? You're obsessed with sex, aren't you, David? You like looking at pornographic pictures on the Internet and you added to your collection by taking photographs of the two girls as well as spying on them.

'Dr Cochrane found out about that, didn't he? He was outraged and, as a result, punished you by immobilizing the very impressive and superior train set-up in the loft, which you value so much, by cutting off the electrical supply. Our people restored the power yesterday, but unfortunately someone, who doesn't like you, or perhaps even more than that, hates you, appears to have smashed most of it up with a sledgehammer.'

Sarah glanced in Sergeant Bristow's direction and nodded. He reached behind himself and lifted up the plastic bag, taking out the twisted metal object from inside. The boy stared for a moment at the mangled remains of the express railway engine, then stared at Amy across the room for a moment before letting out an unearthly scream and getting to his feet.

'You did that, didn't you, you bitch?' he shouted. 'I'll kill you, just like I killed James.'

He launched himself at her across the room, but had only got halfway towards her when his arm was caught in a grip of iron and twisted up behind his back.

'That's quite enough of that, son,' Bristow said. 'Calm down!'

He didn't, continuing to struggle, shouting and screaming as the burly sergeant handcuffed him and bundled him out of the room.

There was a stunned silence in the room and Sarah walked across to Sinclair and whispered in his ear. He nodded and went out of the room, along the corridor where Bristow was holding the boy face down on the table with one massive hand and with his phone in the other.

'I've just sent for a van, sir.'

'Good man. Have you cautioned him yet?'

'Yes, sir, and he just swore at me.'

Sinclair nodded. 'I have just one very short task before he goes.'

He plunged his hand into the boy's trouser pocket, found the crumpled cotton garment and left the room, handing it to Sarah while shielding it from Rebecca Cochrane, who was still sitting, white-faced on the settee. Sarah managed to get Rebecca on her own as she was leaving and gave it to her.

The young women flushed slightly. 'I can't tell you how grateful I am to you. Should one of the tabloids have got hold of this, my life at the hospital would have been a misery. No, I'm not exaggerating. I've spent practically all my medical career at St Gregory's Hospital, I was also a student there, and I can reasonably expect to get a consultant post very soon as there are some retirements coming up. St Gregory's is still quite inbred and there are lots of people there who don't like me. Why? It's because there was a cult of sex, drinking and soft drug taking in my student time and I would have none of it. I was known as a goody-goody, a kill-joy, and a humourless, sexless robot. Some of those people are still about and if it got known that a pair of my panties had been found in the trouser pocket of my father's murderer, not only would the press have had a field day, they would never have left it alone, I just know they wouldn't.'

'Don't worry, the only people who know about it are me and my partner, Mark Sinclair, and I promise you that it will never go any further. You may trust both of us completely, not least because both of us suffered in a minor way from that sort of thing earlier on in our careers.'

'Thank you again. What's going to happen to David now?'

'It all depends whether he is considered fit to plead. I will let you know as soon as a decision has been taken.'

CHAPTER ELEVEN

'I THOUGHT IT was time to have a word with Tredgold about this case,' Tyrrell said, when he had summoned his two assistants to his office a few weeks later. 'For once, though, I've decided that he should play away.'

To Sinclair's amusement, away from his home patch, the forensic pathologist hadn't got quite his usual edge, but that wasn't entirely the case.

'Firstly,' Tyrrell said when they were seated with coffee and biscuits having been distributed, 'as usual, Eric, you were quite right.'

'Usual?' the man said, 'not always?'

Tyrrell wasn't in the least put out. 'Usual, quite definitely. I am referring, in this instance, to your experiment in determining that the strength required for wielding that stone would not have been very great. David Moffatt could reasonably be described as weedy and had it not been for you, suspicion might have been deflected from him. However, what we really wanted to ask you was your opinion on the future for the boy, as I remember that you had experience of prison medicine early in your career. As you know, the boy is at present in a secure psychiatric unit, having been found unfit to plead by reason of insanity. However, as we suspect that after quite a short time he may start to behave himself, how long do you suppose he'll be kept there, in a young offenders' unit or in prison?'

'That will depend on whether the cause of his insanity is determined and if it is considered to be of a temporary or permanent nature. His age is obviously a major factor and my best guess is that he may well come to trial in front of a jury, depending on how he behaves in the secure mental hospital where he is at present. The verdict, from all I've heard about this case, is likely to be guilty, but the sentence may be qualified by consideration of temporary insanity, and his age will be taken into account as well. He may, of course, be detained where he is now if he is psychotic and deemed to be a danger to himself and others. All in all, should he settle down, I wouldn't be surprised if he gets out within a few years.'

'If that happens, do you think he will remain a serious risk, particularly as far as Amy Moffatt is concerned. He threatened her very directly in our hearing?'

'I have no means of knowing and that is what makes these cases so difficult. As you obviously know, before I took up forensic pathology, I was a prison doctor for some time and prediction in cases like this is an inexact science, to say the least. I must say I feel for the forensic psychiatrists who have to make the decision. If they recommend that he is eventually released and he does behave acceptably in the future, no one is going to praise them, but should he attack or murder someone else, all hell will descend on their shoulders. Rather them than me.'

'What are your views, Sarah and Mark?'

'We have discussed it at length and have little to add to what Dr Tredgold has said,' Sarah replied. 'One thing we do believe, though, and that is if he is released, Amy Moffatt would be well advised to make herself very scarce indeed, even to the extent of emigrating.'